Bad Company

S.L. STERLING

Bad Company

Copyright © 2019 by S.L. Sterling

All rights reserved.

Without limiting the rights under copyright reserved about, no part of this publication may be reproduced, stored in, or introduced into a retrieval system, or transmitted in any form or by any means (mechanical, electronic, photocopying, recording, or otherwise) without the prior written permission of both the copyright owner and the above publisher of the book. This is a work of fiction. Any references to historical events, real people, or real places are used fictitiously. Other names, characters, places, and events are products of the author's imagination, and any resemblance to actual events or places or persons, living or dead, is entirely coincidental. Disclaimer: This book contains mature content not suitable for those under the age of 18. It involves strong language and sexual situations. All parties portrayed in sexual situations are consenting adults over the age of 18.

Editor: Missy Borucki

Cover Design: Sarah Paige, Opium House Creatives

Interior Formatting: Lee Ching, Under Cover Designs

ISBN: 978-1-9995736-2-1

PROLOGUE

I stood in the hallway fiddling with my lock. It was only the second month of high school and I had already forgotten how to work it—again. If my father had to replace it a third time due to my inability to remember my combination, I was sure to be in trouble. I had English in five minutes and needed to get my books.

"Dammit, this lock won't open again," I said more to myself than to Jenna who stood at her locker beside me. I let out a deep sigh and began again.

"That's because you are doing it wrong. Rotate clockwise, then counter-clock wise then clockwise again. You are also putting in the wrong combination twelve–forty–ten." I looked over at her, annoyed as she shrugged her shoulders and let out a small laugh the more frustrated, I got.

We heard a bunch of loud voices approaching from down the hall causing Jenna to look. "Don't look now, but here comes your boyfriend," Jenna sang as I finally got my lock to open with ease thanks to her help.

I glanced down the hall my lock in hand as the group approached, a funny flutter in my stomach. "It's not fair that someone looks that good this early in the morning," I whispered to Jenna referencing the girl he had his arm wrapped around.

Cindy Reilly, captain of the cheerleading squad, had been dating him for the past year. Rumor had it they were on the outs; she had gone away with her family over summer and he had apparently dated two other girls from school during that time. "I heard they may break up after school today," Jenna whispered. "Then you can date him."

I let out a laugh at her suggestion. "Yeah right, look at her, look at me. He would never be interested." I half-listened to what she said next, I couldn't tear my eyes from him. He was hot, his backpack slung over his broad shoulder. His dark brown hair hung in the way of his crystal blue eyes. With his arm flung over her shoulder, his t-shirt had ridden up and his jeans hung low enough to not only give me a peek at his Calvin Klein boxers but also his solid abs. He seriously reminded me of a model in one of those ads.

I continued to stare as they approached and finally, just as they passed, he dropped his arm from Cindy and turned to stare at me as he walked backward down the hall, winking in my direction before one of the other guys from the football team hit him in the arm. They all let out a roaring laugh at something he said and then opened the door at the end of the hallway, descending the stairs to the hallway below.

"I do believe he just checked you out," Jenna whispered in my ear.

"I doubt that," I mumbled turning to grab my copy of Gatsby and my English notebook now that my morning distraction was gone. I didn't even know his last name.

Earlier in the year, I had gone back into school one afternoon to use the bathroom and had run right into him. He was in full uniform standing outside the guys' locker room just before football practice. He had grabbed my arm before I fell flat on my back, steadying me and saved me from falling. "Whoa there, cupcake, slow down, you all right?" he had said laughing, those blue eyes twinkling. His touch had sent waves of excitement through me. From that day on, I stayed after school every night and watched him from the bleachers in the field.

Jenna and I sat down in our seats in English. The teacher

walked in and I opened my notebook to the notes from last class. I listened with half an ear to the teacher drone on about symbolism in Gatsby, while I doodled his name all over the page —Logan.

1
Logan

Another Saturday night and my mother was on her way out the front door for another date with Joe. It was the tenth Saturday in a row that the same thing was happening. How do I know that it was the tenth Saturday? I had kept count. I won't lie, at first, I thought it was cute that my mother had a date here and there, after all it had been a long time since she had done anything for herself.

When my father died, she had put all her energy and focus into working and looking after me. My mother waitressed at two of the higher end restaurants in town, she worked twelve-hour shifts six days a week just to make sure we had the things we needed. Most days she was so tired she would fall asleep watching TV, sometimes before we even had dinner. Her one day off—always Saturdays—she would spend the day cleaning the house top to bottom, doing the laundry, all while cooking enough food for my lunches to last me the week at school.

I was hanging out with my friends, playing video games, when Mom came down the stairs dressed in a pair of dress pants and a nice sweater and grabbed her coat from the hall closet. "Logan, honey, make sure your friends are on their way home by ten."

"Sure, Mom, Have fun."

I watched as she walked out the door; she looked different, happy, and wore this funny small smile plastered on her lips.

"Where is your mom going, dude? I was hoping she'd make us pizza tonight; I am dying for it. My mom's pizza sucks. She buys those stupid kits—the kind where the crust is like eating cardboard."

"She is going on a date with a guy she's been seeing a lot lately, but she left some money on the table to order one," I answered trying to get back into the game.

"That sounds good," Frank replied.

I got up from the floor and grabbed the phone, pressing the speed dial for the pizza place.

"Do you know this guy?"

"Nope, haven't had the pleasure of meeting him yet and, to be honest, I don't care to."

"Come on, Logan, your mom looks thrilled. You should be happy for her."

I shrugged it off. I was serious that I didn't care to meet this guy. The little I knew about him, I already didn't like him. Meeting him would only make things worse I was sure. "Just play the damn game, I'm getting slaughtered here." Frank picked up his controller and soon we were both involved in the game, pizza was on the way, and within minutes I had forgotten all about my mom and her date.

The next morning, I woke bright and early. I looked at the clock and noted it was only six-thirty. I didn't need to get out of bed for another ten or fifteen minutes, so I rolled back over. I had picked up a small paper route so I didn't have to bother asking Mom for spending cash that I knew she wouldn't be able to give me, things were tight as it was. This job gave me enough money in my pocket every week to do a few things with my friends without putting the strain on my mother, some months I could even help with the grocery bill.

As I lay there staring up at the ceiling, I heard a man's laughter coming from downstairs. Frowning, I sat up, rubbed my eyes and listened again, yep a man's laugh. I grabbed my sweats and made my way down to the kitchen.

I rounded the corner, and that was when I saw Joe for the first time. He had thick dark hair and bulky build. I could tell he was tall too. He was dressed in dress pants and a white shirt that hung open at the neck, his tie draped over the back of my mother's chair. They sat there together, a mug of coffee in front of each of them. My mother's hand rested in his and occasionally he would lift her hand and kiss the back of it, and then he would lean in and whisper something in her ear and she would blush and then let out a laugh. I stood in the doorway taking in this disgusting display of affection when he noticed me watching them. When my mother noticed Joe was looking past her, she turned and smiled. "Morning, honey, you're up early."

"Yeah, have to get the papers out," I mumbled.

"A teenager with initiative, up at the crack of dawn on a Sunday morning." I glared at him as he spoke but said nothing. I went to the fridge and grabbed the orange juice and poured myself a glass.

"Logan, I'd like you to meet Joe," my mother said trying to understand the look on my face.

"Little early for company, isn't it, Mom," I grumbled, heading to the fridge to put the juice back ignoring the fact he held his hand out for me to shake. Suddenly I felt like the parent and Mom was the child, which was ridiculous since I had just turned seventeen.

"Joe's just getting ready to head to work."

"Leaving for work?" I questioned, "What the hell did he do, spend the night?" The embarrassment on my mother's face followed by their uncomfortable silence confirmed what I guessed.

Joe stood and cleared his throat. "Nice to meet you, Logan, and on that cue, Anna, I'm going to go. I'll see you tonight?"

"Yes, seven correct?" He nodded, and I waited as he leaned down and kissed my mother. I glared after him and my mother as she walked him to the door. I didn't like this one bit, there was something about the guy I didn't like.

I had made a bowl of cereal and was on my way over to the table with my bowl and juice in my hand when Mom came back and sat down beside me. I said nothing, instead I shoved food into my face. I could sense her gaze burrowing into my head. "What?"

"Logan, what has gotten into you?"

"I don't know what you're talking about," I murmured.

"Yes, you do! You can't be like that. Joe is a great man, Logan. Give him a chance and get to know him, please."

"Does he know about Dad?" I questioned between mouthfuls. For whatever reason it was important for me to know that. It would determine for me how serious she was about this guy.

"Yes, I told him. He feels bad for you, growing up without a father."

"Honestly, Mom, if you're happy that is all that matters. But I don't need to like him." I stuck my face in my bowl and shoveled more cereal in my mouth. Mom sat there watching me, but I ignored her too and when my bowl was empty, I put it into the dishwasher and went to get dressed.

For the rest of the summer it was Joe at our place or Mom at his. She stopped asking me to get to know him and left me alone. At first it bothered me, but then I realized that with her being busy I could hang with my friends and just do whatever I wanted. When I finally succumbed and got to know Joe a little, he didn't seem like that bad of a guy, but I made it clear I wasn't interested in forming any type of relationship with him. He tried hard to get to know me, but something in me didn't want to become attached to some man.

All that mattered was that he seemed to make Mom happy. I already knew when I got married, I wanted to build the perfect life, for the perfect family, but right now all I was concerned with was getting good grades in school. I had plans to move out of state for college, I even had the school and program picked out. So, if Mom had someone to occupy her time when I moved it was better for me because I wouldn't feel as if I were abandoning her.

It was one of the last few weeks of summer before I was

starting my senior year and I was in the kitchen making my afternoon snack when I heard the front door slam. "Logan, I'm home. Where are you, sweetie?" I heard Mom call from the entryway.

"In here, making a snack." Mom had returned from Mexico with Joe two weeks ago. It had been her first vacation in years and when she returned, she looked more relaxed and refreshed than she had since before my father died. Today was her first day back to work and from the sound of her banging around it hadn't been a good day. She walked into the kitchen and threw her purse on the table flinging her light fall jacket on the back of the chair. The mornings were getting cooler now that September was just about here.

"Do you have dinner planned for tonight, sweetie?" she asked, sitting down and rolling her neck.

I carried my plate over to the table and took one look at my mother. Her tan had faded, and she was already looking worn out. It didn't surprise me since she had no down time—she was either looking after me or spending time with Joe. It was catching up to her as I feared it would.

"I pulled chicken from the freezer. I could throw it on the barbecue," I said shoving a cracker with cheese into my mouth, offering her the plate. It wasn't unlike me to barbecue or cook dinner for us, Mom already did enough.

She shook her head at my offer a smile coming to her lips. "How would you like to go out for a special dinner." I looked at her funny. We never ate out, the only exception being my birthday and that had already passed. We couldn't afford it.

"Mom, is everything all right, you're not sick, are you?" I said shoving another cracker in my mouth and washing it down with a swig of soda, a worried expression crossing my face.

She let out a little laugh. "Heaven's no, it's just Joe and I have special news. We would like to tell you and Leah together." She stood from her chair, rubbed my shoulder as she walked past me and put the kettle on for her afternoon tea.

"Leah? What news?" I said with my mouth full looking over at my mother.

"Yes, Leah, his daughter, remember I told you about her. She's just entering her sophomore year at your school. I've mentioned her to you before. As for what we want to tell you, it's a surprise. We want to tell you both once we get to the restaurant, so get yourself ready. Logan, make sure you dress nicely, we are leaving at six," she said, pulling the box of tea down from the cupboard.

I watched her, she was in her own little world, a small smile plastered on her face. I left my plate on the table and headed upstairs to my room.

I slammed my bedroom door. I knew the man had a daughter, sure we hadn't met yet, but that was because I didn't care to. What news was she talking about? I didn't know what was coming, but I had a feeling it would not be good. I wished she had told me the news here, when I had my mouth full, maybe I would have choked to death, which, to be honest, wouldn't have been such a bad thing.

2
Leah

Summer had passed so quickly, it disappointed me that in only two weeks I would be back sitting in a classroom, staring out a window, wishing that summer was still here, and that Dad and I had spent more time together. Dad had been so busy working and dating Anna since the start of summer, and I had been feeling neglected. We had had all these plans before school had ended, museum trips, camping, day hiking but and not one of them had happened. The only time I had seen my father this summer had been when Anna had been with us. She was a nice lady, but I wasn't used to having to compete for my father's attention.

I had been the apple of my father's eyes since I was born. Dad had fought for custody of me when my mother up and left us. He had won, and I couldn't be happier. My dad worked hard, he owned a used car lot, and his hours were long but no matter what he always made time for whatever I needed. We were comfortable. Then when Anna came into his life things changed. I expressed my displeasure at the lack of my father's attention, but he just laughed at me and asked if I wanted him to be all alone the rest of his life.

We had gotten into the same conversation just the other night. I was irritated, Dad and Anna had just returned from two weeks in Mexico and no sooner had she gone home, she returned and spent the night after Dad had promised me a father and daughter movie night. "Leah, I don't understand what has gotten into you," he said as he marched around the room.

"Daddy, I don't want to share you. We've done nothing this summer, nothing."

"Sure we have, before I left we went to the zoo."

"Yes, we went to the zoo, with Anna," I said emphasizing her name. My father just looked at me as I stomped my foot and threw the book I had been reading down on the table.

"Please, Leah, understand something, I'm thrilled, Anna is like a breath of fresh air compared to your mother."

"Of course she is, Mom is a horrible person. She didn't even call me on my birthday this year."

No matter how much I begged for attention, my father kept telling me I wasn't being put second, and that I was still the most important person in his life.

The next afternoon I was on my way home from my friend's house, riding my bike past the coffee shop just down the road from where Dad's lot was. I stopped and bought Dad a coffee and his favorite donut just like I had done so many times before. I quickly rode down the street and pulled into the car lot. I was hoping to spend time with him alone while he had his coffee. I wanted to talk to him about some back to school shopping I needed to do. I chained my bike and headed into the showroom where Judy the receptionist greeted me, "Afternoon, Leah."

"Hi, Judy, I brought Dad a coffee and donut. Is he in his office?" I asked smiling walking toward his closed door.

"Yes, he is, Anna is speaking with him, dear."

My stomach dropped, and the smile fell from my face. I let out a huff, of course he was. I flopped down in the chair just outside his door and peeked in through the little side window. I saw two coffees sitting on his desk and a brown paper bag.

I continued watching as Dad picked up the brown bag and pulled out a donut, a chocolate glaze, exactly what I had bought him and watched as he shoved it into his mouth. He then shoved a small piece into Anna's mouth and they both laughed at whatever he had said. I rolled my eyes, then looked down at my hands, a coffee sat in one, the brown bag in the other. She had beat me to it, how did she even know it was his favorite snack. I could feel the jealousy pouring out of me.

I turned away, slumped into the chair and listened to their muted laughter. "Judy, can you message my father, please?"

"Sorry, Leah, he has requested that he not be interrupted."

"But it's me, not some stupid customer." I pouted, crossing my arms in front of me and flopping back down on the chair.

She looked up from whatever she was working on and said, "Young lady, he said not to interrupt him for anyone, I'm sorry, Leah, you must wait."

The anger churned inside of me as I continued to sit there listening to their laughter. I wasn't waiting anymore. I got up from the chair and pushed his door open. They both turned, a look of guilt washing across both their faces as if someone had caught them doing something they shouldn't have.

"Leah, how dare you barge in here like that. What if I was with a customer?"

"But you're not, it's just Anna. I brought you a coffee and a donut, thought you might be hungry. It's getting cold, and I know you don't like cold coffee," I said pretending I didn't see the cup and half eaten donut on his desk.

"Thanks, but Anna just brought me one too. I'll keep this one for later." He took the coffee and the donut from my hand and sat them up on his filing cabinet. "Now, Leah, honey, is there an emergency."

I looked between the two of them and shook my head no.

"All right then, I'll be home after the lot closes, and we can talk then."

I couldn't believe what I heard. I was dismissed—my father telling me to go away without saying it. They both stood there looking at me, neither of them said anything. I turned and stomped out of his office, tears threatening to fall. As soon as I got out into the showroom a few people looked my way. Hurt feelings combined with the embarrassment I felt sent me running out the front door and I rode my bike home.

My father never thanked me for the coffee when he got home that night, and I stopped going to the shop after that. I holed up in my room for the rest of the summer, only leaving to do the back to school shopping I needed to get done.

It was the last Friday of the summer, school was starting back on Monday. Before Dad left for work this morning, he told me to be ready when he got home. He didn't say why but Fridays used to be our weekly Daddy—Daughter night. I barely contained my excitement all day. I hoped that we would spend the last Friday of summer together, so I chose a movie to watch and for dinner I thought we could order in, like we normally did. I glanced at the clock, Dad would be home soon. I put my book down, changed into my favorite sweater, grabbed my brush and ran it through my long red hair.

The front door slammed, and I heard Daddy calling my name from the living room. I dropped the brush down on my dresser, threw my hair up in a ponytail and ran down the stairs.

"Hey, Daddy." I ran up and wrapped my arms around him giving him the biggest hug. It was rare that he was home without Anna. "I have the movie all picked out, I was just about to place an order from China King."

"We're not staying in, my love," Dad said pulling me against him.

I pulled out of his embrace and looked up at him. "What do you mean?"

"Well, we are meeting Anna and her son, Logan, for dinner."

I felt that familiar little friend, jealousy, creeping back into my body and I couldn't help the discouraged look that came across my face. I was less than thrilled about spending any more time with Anna. I was tired of all my father's time being monopolized by her.

"Why? I thought this was supposed to be our night." I stomped my foot. Another surge of jealousy ran through me. I was my father's princess, had been since I was born. I didn't want to share him with her anymore, I'd shared him all summer.

"Leah, listen, I have been alone for a long time. I'm happy, and let's be honest and serious for a moment, you will not be around forever. Once you're done high school, the whole world will be in front of you. I'm sure you will move out—maybe even out of the city—then what will I do. This is a good thing for me, Leah."

"Why does this dinner have to happen tonight?"

I watched him take in a deep breath before he spoke. When his eyes met mine, I knew something bad was coming. "We have something we want to tell you both at the same time."

"What if I don't want to go?" I crossed my arms and took a step back.

"Leah, you are going!" He looked at me, but I glared back.

"I'm not having dinner with her and her son. End of story." I flopped down on the couch and turned on the TV.

"Young lady, get yourself up. You don't want to eat, that is fine, but we are going. You will be pleasant this evening too, understand? I won't have it any other way, now let's go."

I didn't move, I could feel the tears building in my eyes as my father looked at me and said, "I will be in the car, you have five minutes."

Dad turned and walked out the front door, he was serious. I sat there for the full five minutes until I saw my father get out of the car and start making his way toward the front door. I knew if he came into this house to get me I would be grounded. So I got up, locked the front door and joined my father in the car.

"Logan, honey, this is Leah. Joe is just out parking the car," said my mother.

I looked up from my phone. I recognized her instantly, the same girl who for the past year had stared at me every morning as I made my way back to my locker, and who sat in the bleachers every football practice. She was the prettiest girl I had ever seen. Her long red hair framed her face and fell softly down her back, her green eyes stood out against her dark black sweater. She had perfectly bowed lips and a cute button nose.

"Hi, Logan," she said smiling back at me.

I didn't answer instead I glared at my mother, pretending I didn't want to be here even though I wanted nothing more than to sit and stare at Leah all night. "How long do we have to be here?"

My mother's face dropped, I could tell I disappointed her in my behavior. "Logan, sit up straight and put that phone away right now. You will be here as long as I determine," she said through clenched teeth and sat down.

Joe approached the table and sat down beside my mom which meant I had no choice but to sit beside Leah. I watched as he leaned in and kissed my mother before opening his menu. "What you going to have, Logan?" Joe asked.

"I'm not hungry," I said shoving my menu off to the side.

My mother took one look at me and stood up. "Please excuse us for a moment."

I could feel all eyes on me as I got up and followed my

mother outside. As soon as we were out of earshot from people walking into the restaurant, she turned toward me. "Logan, I will not tell you again to smarten up. You are doing a fantastic job of making yourself look foolish."

"I don't want to be here. I don't like him, Mom, and I couldn't care less about Leah."

"Well, in life you have to go places you don't want to go. So, you have ten minutes to change your mind, Logan. I've had enough. You can either eat dinner with us, or you can sit in the car alone until I'm finished. Either way, you will be here until I go home." She didn't give me a chance to respond, instead she walked into the restaurant leaving me standing outside. I could see the embarrassment and disappointment all over her face and that was one thing I didn't like to see. I never disappointed Mom, until now.

I took the full ten minutes to calm myself down before walking back inside. As I made my way back to the table, I saw her green eyes watching me. "You better now?" Leah whispered, leaning into me just enough that I caught a whiff of her perfume. "I don't want to be here either if that makes it better."

"It doesn't and I'm fine," I said and sat down and opened the menu.

She averted her eyes from me and the beautiful smile she had flashed at me quickly fell from her face as she continued looking at the menu.

Once we had finished dessert, and they had refilled the coffee, Joe sat back and took hold of my mother's hand. He looked at both me and Leah and smiled. "So, Anna and I have something we want to share with you both."

"So, share it," I mumbled under my breath, "You've kept us here for over an hour and a half." Mom glared at me, the look from her I knew all too well. Leah giggled.

"I have asked Anna to marry me." As soon as the words left Joe's mouth my eyes shot up from the floor. "She has said yes."

I felt like my world just spun out of control at a million

miles per hour.

"We are getting married next Saturday, we don't want to wait any longer. I know for both of you this will be a big change."

Leah looked at me, she looked no happier about it than I did. "Where are we going to live?" she asked twirling her finger in her hair.

"Anna and I have been looking, and we have put an offer in on a house across town. We should know in a few days, it's a nice four-bedroom home. Neither of the houses we own now can't accommodate all of us."

"We're moving?" Leah gasped. "I don't want to move."

"Leah, it's not the end of the world, it will be a good move," Joe said.

I sat there listening as they droned on and on about how in love they were. They were getting married in front of the JP, blah blah blah. Leah sat there looking just as disturbed as I was. As soon the check arrived and this torturous dinner was finally at its end, I excused myself to go outside to wait. I had just walked out the front door of the restaurant when I heard my name.

I turned around and saw Leah striding toward me. "I'm not thrilled about this either. Maybe we could be friends?" she said those green eyes looking up at me.

How could I be friends with this girl? When I had seen her for the first time I had instantly gotten hard. "We shall see." That was all I had time to say because Mom and Joe were coming.

"You kids getting along okay?" Joe asked.

I said nothing before I climbed into the car and slammed the door. Mom kissed Joe goodbye and finally climbed into the car. As we reversed out of the spot, I saw Leah sitting in the front seat of their van; she smiled and waved. I scowled back. We drove home in utter silence.

I wasn't happy about any of this—the wedding or moving in with Joe and Leah. I needed to make that little girl's life a living hell, because if I didn't, there would be no way I could live at home for the next year and keep my hands to myself.

I sat in my now empty room, nothing could have prepared me for all of this. A wedding, a new stepmother, the guy I had a massive crush on is my new stepbrother and to top it off now we had to move. Seemingly overnight everything had changed. It was no longer just Dad and me.

After Dad and Anna told us at dinner and ruined Logan's and my life, they were married in front of a JP the following weekend just as they had said they would be. Two weeks later, they got word that their offer was accepted, and the new house was theirs. Dad hired a company to come in and pack up both houses.

Dad had sold the only home I had ever known and now I had to say goodbye before starting a new life on the other side of town. I looked at the four walls of my bedroom, tape marks from the posters I had hung sat there. In a split second I went from loving my life to hating everything about it. The only thing I was even the slightest bit happy about was that I now had an older brother.

My best friend, Jenna, had an older brother, and he always protected her, always looked out for her, and I was hoping it would be the same for me. Logan, however, didn't seem too thrilled with this arrangement, but I was still hoping that we would become good friends.

"I want you to be on your best behavior Leah. Anna has been having issues with Logan. Don't make this difficult," Dad said as he took a sip of the coffee he had stopped to get before we followed the moving truck across town to the new house.

I scowled, he did not understand how I felt about all this, because he hadn't asked me. I was so angry at him for not talking about all this first, but I kept my mouth shut. When we pulled into the driveway, the first thing I saw was Anna. She was struggling with a box trying to pull it from the back of her van. Dad put the car in park and jumped out shouting at Anna to leave the box that he would get it. She turned and gave us a wave and a big smile, I waved back as I climbed out of the car.

As soon as Dad got to her, he wrapped her in his arms and kissed her pulling him against him. "Everything going okay?" he asked her.

"As well as it can be I guess," she said.

"Is he still acting up?"

Anna was just about to say something when Logan rushed out of the garage, walked over to the van and tore the box from the back of the vehicle, ripping a hole through the side of Anna's box of cleaning supplies. "I told you I got it, Mom."

"Hi, Logan," I said trying to smile even though I felt like crap.

He said nothing, instead he scowled at my father and turned toward the house taking the box with him.

"Good morning, Leah," Anna said, "I told Logan he had to wait to pick his room until you got here." I nodded and went back over to the car to grab two bags I packed last minute.

"Has he been this grumpy all morning?" I heard my dad ask.

"I think he is just trying to adjust. What about Leah?"

"She's been quiet but other than that I think she is doing okay." I watched as he kissed her again, talking about me like I wasn't even here.

As I walked by them, I smiled and headed inside and upstairs. The movers were already in the master bedroom assembling the furniture. Why was it they got to choose their bedroom first? I checked out the first bedroom—it had hardwood floors and there was only one small window and it faced out the side of the house. I ventured to the second bedroom, this one was much bigger and had three large windows. It had a dark blue carpet, not suitable for a girl but maybe Logan would like it I thought. There were already boxes in the room, so I was sure that Logan must have taken it. When I poked my head into the last bedroom, I was in love. It was spacious, not as big as the one with the blue carpet but bigger than my old room. The large windows faced out the front of the house and I could see the tops of the lilac bushes. I could almost smell the lilacs now and it had a pink carpet. I had always wanted a room with a pink carpet.

I was just about to yell down to Dad and Anna when Logan came rushing past me carrying a large box. He placed it on the floor, reached into the box and pulled out a poster. As he unrolled it a half-naked girl appeared, and he hung it the far wall. He walked across the room toward me with another poster in his hand. He unrolled it and tacked it into the wall. As he reached up his shirt rose allowing his abs to peek out. He had a splattering of hair that led down into his jeans, and they hung low enough and I could see a well defined "V". I swallowed hard, and I said nothing, I stood and watched him as he walked back toward the box to get another poster. "Get out, this is my room." I heard him grumble under his breath.

"What do you mean, your room? Your mom just told me that you were told to wait to choose until I got here."

"Well, you're here, and I'm claiming this one," he said pointing to the poster he'd just hung up. He grinned at me and rummaged through the box again.

"But this is a girl's room, it has a pink rug. I figured you would want the one with the blue rug."

He walked across the room toward me and stopped right in front of me, his six-foot frame towering over me and looked right into my eyes. I smelled his cologne and my breath caught —he smelled good enough to eat. I knew my eyes probably betrayed me, but I kept focused on his anyway. "You figured wrong. I like pink, besides, unless you like half naked women, I'll be keeping this room."

I could feel the burn of irritation run through me. "Logan," I choked out.

"Is that it? You like half naked women, then be my guest." He held his hand out opening it to the room. I didn't move, between the smell of his cologne and the heat coming off his body it was like I was glued to my spot.

"Well," his deep voice asked, "are you staying or going?" His eyes stared into mine, his tongue jutting from his mouth to wet his kissable lips.

"Have you picked out your rooms?" I heard Dad ask from below. I ripped my eyes from Logan's, stepped back and walked into the room across the hall. While Logan went back to his box of naked women, I went downstairs to get my bags. I figured it was just easier to let him have the room than to fight for it.

The rest of the day passed by, and I stayed in my room setting things up. Once the movers left, they called us down for dinner. We sat at the table, Dad at the head, Anna across from him and Logan and I across from one another. Logan glared at me while swirling his fork around in his pasta. When I made eye contact with him he stuck his tongue out at me.

"You kids all settled into your new rooms? I will admit, Leah, I am kind of surprised that you didn't take the room Logan chose," my father said digging into his dinner.

I was just about to tell them what happened when Logan gave me a look and kicked me under the table. I jumped and my knee hit the bottom of the table causing everything to rattle.

"Leah, are you okay?" Anna asked. Dad looked up from his plate and gave me a questioning look.

I looked at Logan who was grinning at me. "I bit my lip," I lied. "Yep, all settled in," I answered my dad before going back to eating my dinner.

"So, Anna, when do you go back to work?" I asked between mouthfuls.

"Well, your father and I talked about it. We have decided that I'm needed here at home more. So, I gave my notice last week and completed my last shift before the move."

I noticed Logan perked up and was now keenly listening to what was being said.

"You will be here like all the time?" I questioned.

"Yes. I used to love to cook, we will have some amazing meals for dinner because I can be home. I think you will love some of my deserts, dear. I make a great chocolate fudge cake, just ask Logan."

I looked at my father who sat with his hand over hers. "We are looking forward to it, Anna," he said as he winked. Dad used to love my deserts too, before her, that was.

"I make a good cake too, right, Dad," I asked.

"Yep, not bad, but I bet you could take lessons from Anna." I took a sip of water to help swallow the lump that was forming in my throat and forced to keep the tears unshed.

"What about college?" I asked.

"What about it?"

"Well, if Anna isn't working, how will you pay for us both to go to school, Daddy." Bottom line was I had been told I could go anywhere I wanted. Now with two of us to pay for, if that was going to change, she needed to work.

"The dealership is doing well. There is nothing to worry about, Leah, everything will stay as is. Same goes for you too, Logan."

I breathed out a sigh and was just about to say something when I heard Logan clear his throat.

"May I be excused?" Logan asked.

"Logan, you barely ate anything," Anna said looking worried. "Are you not feeling well?"

"I'm not hungry." He didn't wait, he pushed himself away from the table and headed upstairs.

I helped Anna with the dishes and then spent the rest of the evening watching TV with Anna and Dad. At 9:30 I made my way up to my room. I had school tomorrow and I was tired. Trudging up the stairs, I walked into my room to find Logan sitting on my bed with my diary open in his hand. He looked up from the page he was reading and gave me a sly smile.

"Give me that!" I shouted practically running across the room. I went to grab my diary from him, but he stood up and held it over his head. It was impossible for me to reach.

"Oh, Gingersnap, why? Don't want me to know about Aaron or Matt, guess you're not into girls after all," he said looking down into my face.

I shoved him against the wall and tried to reach for my diary once again. "Don't call me that, give me my diary back."

"Don't call you what?"

"You know what!"

"You better be careful, Gingersnap, I wouldn't want you to get turned on by pressing up against me like you did when Aaron accidentally brushed against you in gym class." He laughed grabbing hold of me, wrapped his arm around my back and pulled me against him while he ground his hips into me.

My cheeks burned with embarrassment and I pulled away. "Give me my diary back, Logan."

"You know there is a lot of great material in here." I watched as he flipped to another page and read the lines I had written. Tears were threatening to pour down my cheeks as I finally ripped the diary from his hands.

Logan chuckled to himself. "Oh, Gingersnap, it's all right, don't worry, I won't tell anybody." He laughed and walked out of the room, as he crossed the hall he repeated what he had read.

I slammed my door shut and hid my diary in one of my drawers. Thank god he had started at the front and not the more recent entries, I would have died if he read about him. I got ready for bed, cracked open my bedroom door, crawled under the covers and opened the book I had been reading. A while later I heard Logan talking to one of his friends.

"Yeah, I took the damn room, I fucking hate the color pink." I could feel the anger boil in me, he had done it on purpose. "I only took it because then she couldn't have it. Yeah, I know, I expected her to cry like a little girl too."

I threw my book down, got up, slammed my door shut and crawled into bed pulling the covers up over my head. I hated everything about this move.

The rest of the week I tried my best to ignore what had happened and what I had heard, and Logan barely looked at me again, never mind mentioning anything else. The following Friday, Dad and Anna left for a weekend away with friends, which meant Logan and I were alone together for the first time.

"Now please tell me you two won't kill one another while we're gone," Dad said as he grabbed Anna's coat from the hall closet right before they left.

"No, sir. I'm just gonna play my video games, and I'm sure Leah will do whatever girly things she normally does. You know, write in her diary, cry over some guy."

I walked into the living room carrying a bowl of popcorn and a can of soda and sat down in the living room chair across from Logan, ignoring his snarky commentary. "When will you be back, Dad?" I asked picking up my book.

"Sunday morning. Oh, and for tomorrow night's dinner, I left you guys money for pizza," Anna said. She kissed us both on the top of the head and then walked out the door with my father.

A while later I sat munching on popcorn, texting with Jenna, ignoring the idiot across the way from me who sat there engrossed in his stupid video game. After an hour, Logan shut the game off, and we watched a stupid show about deep sea fishing.

"Hey, Gingersnap, what's your phone number and your email address?"

"What do you want those for?" I had given up about asking him not to call me that, the more he knew I hated it the more he used it. It wasn't just the nickname I hated, I had hated the color of my hair since I was a child, so it bothered me that he called me that.

"Well, if you ever need a ride home, you can text me. Seriously, I think it's time we buried the hatchet."

"Only if you promise not to call me Gingersnap."

"No problem, Leah." He smiled at me.

I was leery, but we exchanged information and for one night out of the few we had lived in the same house we sat and watched a movie together without arguing.

Three weeks later I came home and threw my book bag down on the kitchen table and went upstairs to get my laptop. I had a ton of homework to finish. Anna made me a hot cup of tea and a snack while I opened my textbooks and began working away. I was just about to email one of my friends about an assignment when an email caught my eye.

The subject line was "I like black panties." I frowned looking over my shoulder to make sure that Anna couldn't see my screen before I opened it. Inside was a picture of an older, gross looking man requesting to see a picture of me in a black thong. I scrolled to the bottom of the email and saw that it was sent to Gingersnap16. I felt the rage coil through my veins, no doubt Logan had something to do with this. Suddenly Anna walked into the room and I slammed my laptop down, looked up at her and tried to smile innocently, guilt written all over my face.

"Leah, honey, everything okay?"

"Yes. I was uh, just working on a surprise for your birthday." I smiled up at her.

"Oh, all right, well, I don't want to ruin that." She smiled and refilled her mug with hot water and went back into the living room, sat in her rocker and continued reading her book.

As soon as Anna was gone I picked up my cell phone and sent off a text to Logan.

ME: WHAT DID YOU DO?

Almost instantly a reply came in, like he had been waiting all day for my message.

LOGAN: NOTHING WHY

ME: GINGERSNAP16

LOGAN: OH THAT . . . FIGURED YOU WANTED A DATE AT SOME POINT IN YOUR YOUNG LIFE

ME: DELETE IT NOW OR GIVE ME THE PASS-WORD TO GET RID OF IT

LOGAN: SORRY I CAN'T DO THAT

ME: WHY NOT

LOGAN: WHAT FUN WOULD THAT BE GINGERSNAP

ME: DELETE IT OR I TELL YOUR MOTHER

LOGAN: GO AHEAD SHE WON'T BELIEVE YOU

I threw my phone on the table and opened my laptop back up only to see five more emails in my inbox from different guys. I clicked on the name Gingersnap16 and waited for the page to load. I almost died when the page populated. The photo was one of me in the bathroom after a shower, standing with a towel wrapped around my body. How he had taken it I had no idea but when I read what was on the page, tears starting to pour down my cheeks. I put my head into my hands and called Anna.

"What is it, dear?"

"Look!" I said pointing at my screen. "Logan did this. He set up a fake profile under my name and now all these gross men are messaging me. I asked him to delete it and he said he won't."

Logan came walking through the front door and Anna quickly pulled him into the kitchen. "What on earth do you think you are doing, Logan?"

"Ginger, I mean Leah, needs a boyfriend, so I thought I

would help her out," he said grinning at me, completely giving himself away.

"Get rid of it, Logan, now," she demanded. "This is unacceptable."

"Oh, Mom, relax, it was just a joke," he said laughing.

"A joke? Look at the things these men are saying in their emails. This isn't funny, Logan, it's dangerous. Joe will be beside himself."

Logan grabbed my laptop, turned it toward him, logged into the account and deleted it while Anna watched. "Happy now," he bit out and then took off to his room.

"I'm sorry, Anna," I whispered.

"Oh, honey, don't be silly. It's not your fault.

After I had calmed down, Anna went back to sit in her chair. I continued with my homework, but I realized that Logan would hate me more after this. I would need to dig deep to forgive him because I was determined to make him like me.

5

It had been six months of pure torture sleeping across the hall from her every night. She was part of every masturbatory event I had and even though I treated her like shit almost every single day, all the girl did was continue to try and suck up to me. I figured after the hair dye incident she would stay far away, but no. Shortly after that she baked me a batch of my favorite cookies. I told her they were dry, even though I would secretly sneak down into the kitchen every night after everyone was in bed to eat them.

For my birthday she made me my favorite cake, triple chocolate brownie. Even though it killed me, I only ate one piece of the perfectly moist cake before announcing I was giving up chocolate.

It didn't matter what I did, she kept coming back for more punishment. One night, I replaced her shampoo with lube. She screamed for my mother to help her and while I listened to her as she cried in the bathroom, Joe had come in to have a long talk with me. After he left, I couldn't help but sit there and laugh.

The best prank I pulled was hiding the pregnancy test in her room after she had started dating Aaron. My mother found it while collecting her laundry and I got to stand on the sideline and listen while Joe and Anna had a very serious talk with Gingersnap. It was the funniest thing ever to hear her plead her case to them both that nothing was going on.

Leah barely spoke to me for a month after that. Every time

she would look at me she would get this super cute annoyed look on her face. I won't lie, I was sort of beginning to miss her.

"Are you hanging out with us tonight?" Trevor asked as I walked from the front of the school to my car.

"No, I can't, it's my stepsister's birthday," I said making an annoyed face. "I've been told I have to be home."

I opened the car door and threw my bag in the back.

"Have you heard anything back from the university?"

"Yeah, I got my acceptance a week ago. I haven't told anyone yet. I need to because the tuition will be due soon. Just not sure how my mom will react knowing I am moving across the country."

I looked across the parking lot and saw Leah standing against the tree waiting for the bus. She stood there with her coat pulled tight around her. I kept my eyes on her, there was something about the way she stood there that was bothering me. Normally she was surrounded by her friends but today it was just her, and then Aaron approached her. She turned away from him as he tried to pull her around to face him.

Trevor looked in the direction I was looking. "I don't know how you do it."

"How I do what?"

"Live with that, your stepsister is so fucking hot. If she were mine, I'd be taking every chance I got to sneak into her room at night and tap it."

Every muscle in my body tensed at his comment. "What did you just say?"

"What? I said if she were my stepsister, I would tap that every chance I got."

I turned to him and grabbed him by the collar. "Don't ever let me hear you say anything like that again. You got me." My pulse was hammering in my ears.

"Yeah, man, no problem. Sorry." Trevor held his hands up in defense.

"Listen, I've got to go." I released Trevor and got in my car and started the engine, then turned and looked in her direction again. Aaron flipped her the bird, and I watched him run off. She slumped down against the tree and put her head in her hands.

I drove over and pulled up alongside the road. "Want a ride, Gingersnap?" I yelled from the window.

"Go away, Logan, I'll take the bus," she yelled back.

I wasn't about to beg, so I put the car in drive and headed home.

I had just finished wrapping the special gift I would give to her later when I heard the front door slam and footsteps on the staircase. I poked my head around the corner to see a trail of red hair fly into her room and the door slam. I was about to knock when Mom caught my eye, waving at me to come down into the kitchen. "Logan, Joe will be home soon, come help me in the kitchen for a minute, please."

I followed her in and looked around the room. She'd blown up pink balloons and they surrounded the chair where Leah always sat. Gifts were wrapped, sitting off to the side. "Take the casserole out of the oven, please, while I finish up the decorations on the cake." I watched as she carefully placed the last few roses on the top of the cake.

"What are we having?"

"It's a broccoli casserole. Joe said it used to be Leah's favorite when she was younger, so I found a recipe and made it and for dessert I made a lemon cake."

I pulled the casserole out of the oven and sat it on the counter turning to see Joe walk into the kitchen carrying a small box. "Where is the birthday girl?" he asked walking over and kissing Anna.

"I don't think I've seen her yet this afternoon," Anna said smiling.

"She's upstairs."

"Well, go get her, Logan."

I went up to get her, finding her face down on her bed in

tears. I frowned, why was she crying. "Mom wants you to come down for dinner," I said pushing her door open.

"I'll be there in a minute, go away," was all her muffled voice said.

What seemed like hours later, I was bored to tears while Leah finished opening her gifts, all gifts but mine. I had left it in my room and would give it to her later. While she and Anna were engrossed in looking at the flyer to the spa they were going to over the weekend, deciding what treatments to have, I got to help with dish duty instead of Leah tonight. I felt my phone vibrate in my pocket and grabbed it. Aaron had sent me a text letting me know he had broken up with Leah, and that if she was pissy, it was his fault.

After I put everything away, I wandered up to my room but stopped outside of her door. I could hear more crying and wondered what the hell had happened between them to make her so upset. I grabbed my gift and knocked on her door and waited. I heard a few bangs come from behind the door and then she pulled the door open a crack. She peeked out at me, "What?" I held up the wrapped box in my hand, but taking one look at her I turned around and was going to go back to my room.

"You got me something?" I heard her ask in surprise between sniffles.

"It's nothing, really," I said turning back around still holding the box in my hand. I should have gone with what I had decided, not to give it to her after finding out what had transpired after school. I was being more of an asshole than anything else with what was in the box. I didn't enjoy seeing her like this, and having second thoughts, I turned to walk away again, but she pulled the door open further and invited me into her room.

"No, Logan, please," she said. I turned around and took one look at her, her green eyes sparkling in the light.

I seriously debated just telling her it was an empty box and retreating to my room, but she stood there begging me with those sexy green eyes.

"Please, Logan." I hesitated and then I held the box out to her. She took the box from my hands, went over to her bed and sat down and gently pulled at the purple ribbon. There was no stopping her now. She lifted the edge toward her and gently opened the box only to slam it shut again, her face going as red as her hair, tears filling her eyes.

"Leah, honey, what is it?" I turned and saw Joe and Mom standing behind me on their way to their room. I was going to be up shit's creek now.

"It's just a little private joke between Logan and me," she muttered pushing me into the hall, slamming the door shut on us. I could feel the anger coming from both Mom and Joe as they stood there staring at me.

"Why the hell can you two not get along?" Joe demanded standing behind my mother.

"I'll talk to her." I watched Mom go to Leah's door and open it, slipping inside. Joe stood staring at me as he waited to find out what the hell happened.

Within minutes Mom appeared, closing the door to Leah's room quietly and looked at me with disappointment. "Logan, how could you?"

I shrugged my shoulders and headed into my room, Joe and Mom following me. Apparently, they didn't find the purple vibrator as funny as I had, and I soon found myself grounded.

"Seriously, it was meant as a joke, nothing else," I called as they both walked out of my room.

"You're still grounded," my mom replied.

"Oh, and Logan, tell that to Leah, not to us. I've had enough of this—whatever it is between you two. It needs to stop and now," Joe said before he shut the door to their bedroom.

6
Logan

I finally had to tell Mom and Joe about school. The university had written me twice asking if I would accept. Telling my mom that I was accepted by Boston University into their architecture program was easier than I thought it would be. She and Joe paid for my whole first year with no complaint. I picked up a job bartending at the beginning of summer and had saved enough for my flight in the first couple of weeks and was now working on saving for living expenses.

Mom and I had flown to Boston to check out the dorms on campus and made all the necessary arrangements for moving in for the year. There was a mandatory two-week new student orientation, and I planned to spend the last days of summer getting to know the city and my new roommate before classes started. I seriously couldn't be more excited to get out of here.

I spent the day getting ready for my flight to Boston on the following Monday. I was stuffing a few sweaters into my duffel bag when I heard a knock on my door. I looked up and Leah came wandering in.

"I hope you know I'm claiming this room once you leave."

"Did someone say something?" I asked looking around the room. Leah sat on the edge of my bed, twirling her finger in her long red hair and rolled her eyes at me. Since her birthday we had been getting along, no more mean pranks.

"I will miss you."

"Gingersnap, don't go getting all sentimental on me, you

know damn well you're going to be happier without me around here."

"That's not true," she said looking up at me.

"Need I remind you of the purple vibrator I got you for your birthday, or the pregnancy test I hid." I chuckled. "If you miss me, you are more fucked up than I thought."

She got quiet and then asked, "What time do you leave?"

"Flight is at nine Monday morning. Mom is taking me to the airport. If you want this room, go ahead, it's yours," I said looking around the room. Fucking pink carpet, I couldn't believe I had spent an entire year living in a room with a pink carpet.

"Can I come?"

"Nope, I asked that it just be me and Mom, so whatever goodbyes you need to say, it will have to be done here."

I grabbed a couple of things and threw them into my carry-on bag, leaving only my laptop on my desk. Suddenly I felt her arms wrap around my center, and her body press tightly against my back. The heat of her touching me went straight to my cock, and it jumped in response. There were no words exchanged between us and as quick as she had pulled her body into mine, she let me go, running from my room.

It was Thursday night, Joe and Mom had gone away again for the weekend but promised to be home late Saturday night or early Sunday morning to spend the day with me.

I had been at work for three hours and was busy pouring drinks for the people waiting in line when I saw Leah walk in with Jenna and two guys I didn't recognize. At closer inspection these guys looked to be in their late twenties. What the hell were they doing? Leah had told Joe and Mom she would be home studying all weekend.

I watched as the girls slid into the booth first on opposite sides of the table and then the guys slid in beside them. As soon as the line at the bar got to a manageable level, I excused myself for a moment and moved toward their table. Jenna waved at me as I approached and put my hands on the edge of the table then leaned over toward Leah. "Can I speak to you for a moment, Leah," I asked.

"No, you may not." She rolled her eyes at me and then smiled at Jenna and the two guys.

I ignored the fact she wanted to be left alone. "I thought you were studying all weekend?"

"Plans change. Now, if you don't mind, how about you get us two coolers and two beers?" She tore her eyes away from mine and went about her conversation as if I weren't standing right there.

I stood watching them for a second and then went back behind the bar and got their drinks. I had one of the waitresses take the drinks over to them. As the night went on, I kept an eye on them both, but the later it got the busier it got, and the busier I got until finally I lost track of Leah in the sea of people. Jenna was still sitting at the booth with one guy, so I knew they were still there. When my shift ended, I grabbed my jacket from behind the bar and went over to the table she was at and sat down.

"Logan! Hi." Jeanna beamed.

"Hey, Jenna, where did Leah go?"

"Oh, she is dancing with Tom. They're right over there," she said pointing to a group of dancers. I couldn't see her at first but when the crowd finally parted, I caught a glimpse of her. I saw the way Tom was looking at her and I didn't like it. He looked at her as if she was something to eat instead of a person and that bothered me more than I cared to admit.

"Mind if I sit here with you guys?"

"Nope, not at all," Jenna said smiling.

I pulled my phone from my pocket and scrolled through Instagram, occasionally looking up to see where Leah was. She must have seen me watching her because she finally made her way over with her date to the table. "Hi, Logan."

"You almost ready to go?" I asked. There was just something about this guy that made me uneasy and I decided I wasn't leaving her here with him. Leah had a lot to drink tonight, and he seemed to be too sober.

"It's okay, Logan, Tom will bring me home. Go ahead, you're probably tired, plus I am not ready to leave yet." Tom looked at me and then at Leah and smiled.

"Yeah, Logan, I got her," he said grabbing her ass and pulling her into him.

This wasn't a place to cause a scene, so I decided to just go. "All right then, see you at home."

"Who was that guy? Your boyfriend?" I heard her date yell into her ear over the music. I turned to look at them.

"Just my annoying stepbrother, he thinks he's the boss of me. I hate him." She answered as she looked me right in the eyes.

Her words stabbed at my chest, sure we didn't get along, but hate was an awfully strong word, so I took that as my cue and walked out the front door. As I walked to my car, I realized just how much that comment stung. I unlocked my car and climbed in and was just about to start the engine when I decided to wait until I saw her come out of the bar. I would follow her home, just to make sure she got there okay. I didn't trust that Tom guy.

Two hours went by and finally I saw Jenna and the guy she was with leave the bar, Leah and her date trailing behind. Leah was drunk now, staggering across the parking lot, hanging off him, laughing as she walked. They made it over to what must have been his car where he leaned her against the hood and kissed her. Jenna was already in another car and they left the parking lot. I continued to watch figuring they would leave soon but instead of getting into the car, Tom continued to hold Leah up against the car and they were into a deep make-out session. I watched as he kept grabbing at her, running his hands over her, while she seemed to get agitated, trying to push at his chest to get him away. Suddenly his hand was buried down the front of her pants as she hit at him. I felt my pulse race as he grabbed her hands and held them behind her back as he continued his assault on her.

As anger boiled inside of me, I jumped out of my car and marched across the parking lot. I grabbed him and pulled him off her before punching him right in the mouth, knocking him back. I watched as he fell to the ground then grabbed Leah and pulled her across the parking lot. I put her in my car, got in and drove away. I was glad I had stayed, if I hadn't who knows what would have happened.

The drive home was quiet, she kept her gaze out the window. She had wrapped herself up in my coat, and occasionally, she let out a sob. I pulled the car into the driveway and before I could say anything she jumped out of the car and ran to the door fumbling with her keys and made her way inside. I tapped my thumb on the steering wheel, debating if I should call Joe and Mom, instead of dealing with this on my own. Deciding I wouldn't say anything to anyone, I walked to the front door and once inside I locked it behind me.

I toed my shoes off and went into the kitchen. Like always, I was hungry, so I scrounged around in the fridge and grabbed a mishmash of food to snack on. I picked up my plate and turned to sit at the table when I saw Leah standing inside the kitchen door. She had changed into shorts and t-shirt and had washed all the makeup off her face. She looked better now. "You all right?" I asked.

She nodded and walked past me to the fridge pulling a bottle of water out. "Are you sure?"

"Yes." Her voice shook. She unscrewed the cap from the bottle and took a sip of water. I put my plate down and went back to the fridge for a bottle of water for myself. As I went to walk past her, she grabbed my shirt and leaned in, giving me a kiss on the cheek. "Thank you," she whispered.

I looked down at her, her eyes met mine and she looked me deep in the eyes. It was the first time she had really looked at me in almost four months. Those beautiful green eyes staring back at me, I wished the moment could go on forever. My eyes washed over her face, to her lips and back to those green eyes and as if in slow motion I raised my right hand to her cheek and slowly leaned into her, our lips meeting. For an entire year I had dreamed of kissing those lips and now as we stood in our parents' kitchen, I was kissing her, my stepsister.

As my tongue parted her lips and jutted into her mouth, I felt my cock jump with excitement and harden. I knew she felt it too, because suddenly she pulled away, embarrassment filling her face. Before I could say anything, she ran from the room and I heard her bedroom door slam shut.

7
Logan

I tried to talk to her after I realized what had happened between us. I had called to her from downstairs and even went to her room to try to speak with her, but instead of coming out of her room she asked that I leave her be. So, I jumped into the shower.

I held the towel around my waist but because it was a smaller one, I had to hold both ends closed with my hand. I was just about to my room when Leah shot out of her own room and right into my chest. The contact caused me to jerk backward, losing my grip on the towel.

It fell to the floor leaving me standing there completely naked, her eyes wandered my body. I could see her cheeks get that rosy colored hue to them while her eyes widened as she looked down to my cock. Perhaps she had never seen a naked man before, maybe I was the first. As my eyes washed over her I could see her nipples poking through her tank top and when our eyes met, she cleared her throat and sucked her bottom lip between her teeth.

I took a step toward her leaving my towel on the floor in the hallway and smashed into her lips once again, only this time I let my hands wander, running my palms over her hardened nipples. I was hard as a fucking rock and wanted her to take me in her hands, but she didn't, she kept her hands placed on my chest as if she was going to try and stop me from what I was doing.

As our lips parted, my lips traveled to her neck, and I heard her small voice as she said, "Logan, we can't do this." Instead of pulling away, she continued to kiss me for a minute before she pushed away from me and quickly turned and headed back into her room. Separating us by shutting the door. She left me standing stark naked in the hallway with a raging hard on. I had no idea what I had been thinking, but she was right, this couldn't happen.

When I woke on Saturday, I got dressed and headed down to the kitchen. I had hoped to talk to Leah, so I could apologize and pray to god she didn't speak a word of this to our parents. However, I found a note on the kitchen table telling me she was already up, and she'd gone to stay with Jenna.

Mom and Joe returned home early Sunday morning followed by Leah a little later. We spent the day as a family; we went to church as we did every week where I prayed for forgiveness for what had happened between us. Then like always we went for breakfast. She acted as normal as always, never looking or speaking to me. Although that wasn't the part that hurt the most, Monday morning she didn't even get up to say goodbye before I left.

At first, I thought I had dreamed the whole kiss thing, but as I stood at the airport, I could still taste her and feel her soft lips on mine. Mom stood beside me as we checked the board with all the flight information. "Looks like your flight will be on time," she said pulling me out of my memories.

"Yep." I stood there trying to fight what was eating at me. Aside from Leah occupying my mind, I was suddenly very worried for my mother. I was worried that Joe really couldn't be trusted, and I was concerned for her welfare. I mean once I was gone, who would be there for her if things fell apart.

I stood there watching the flight board fighting back the urge to say anything to her at all.

"You sure you have everything dear?" she asked placing her keys into her purse and sipping from her coffee cup.

I don't know what came over me, but the words fell from my

lips before I could stop them. "Mom, can I tell you something?" I asked her, looking down at the ticket in my hand.

"Of course, sweetie, anything."

I paused still not sure how to tell her what was on my mind. "I'm worried, Mom, about you."

"What? Why?"

I swallowed hard, "What if Joe turns out not to be the man you think he is?"

"What do you mean by that, Logan?"

"Well, it's just you've given up everything, Mom."

She frowned at me. "Logan, I haven't given up everything."

"Yes, you have. As soon as you married and moved in with Joe, you gave up your independence and became the happy little housewife. Look at you."

Mom looked at me, I could see the tears building in her eyes, but I didn't care. I was worried about her and she needed to know it. I wanted her to know that I thought she had made a mistake; people weren't that happy together.

"Look at you. You guys got married and in less than a week you had given up your job, our home, even your car. I mean what happens if he leaves, Mom. Where are you going to go?"

"Logan, that is enough. Joe isn't going anywhere, and I haven't given up anything, I traded it for a better life for us and I have a car. We are in love, Logan, and once you understand what that is you will understand what we have."

"No, Mom, seriously. What if he leaves? I am sure you didn't think Dad would leave."

"Logan, I can assure you Joe is not going anywhere. Your father died, Logan, he didn't choose to leave. You can't even begin to compare the two. Now what has you worried? Are you worried about school?"

"It's just, I'm leaving, what would you do if he left."

"Logan don't be ridiculous. Now your plane . . ."

I cut her off; it wasn't funny. "You walked away from every-thing you used to be and now you have nothing, Mom. Nothing. It's not good, you really shouldn't be so trusting. That's what you always taught me."

"Logan . . ."

I didn't give her a chance to speak. I knew my words hurt, the tears in her eyes told me so. I picked my bag up off the floor and threw it over my shoulder. "I've got to go." I walked away without a hug or another word to my mother and when I had walked through security, I turned around to see her wipe her cheeks from the tears that were now running down them.

I tapped my pen on the edge of my diary.

Summer was ending and soon school would be starting. Since Logan had left, granted it had only been two weeks, things had become routine around the house. I had spent a lot of time alone, not for any reason aside from the fact that I wanted it that way. I was still messed up from that night and I had no one I could talk to about it. I had really wanted to talk to Logan about it, but I was too embarrassed to leave my room before he left. I mean how could you look your stepbrother in the eyes after seeing his little, okay big buddy and getting so turned on that you wanted him to take you right in the hallway. So alone was a good place for me to be.

Dad and Anna would get up early every morning and head down to the water for their morning walk, but I stayed in bed. They tried to get me to go with them a few times but eventually they stopped asking. Then Dad would leave for work and Anna would spend her mornings with her face buried in her books and the afternoon making us delicious meals and deserts.

I had taken an interest in interior design and decorating and had started looking at colleges to attend even though I still had the last year of high-school to complete. I had decided I would go to school in the city so I could live at home. I had purchased a bunch of magazines and Anna had spoken to one of her friends who worked at a firm here and she allowed me to come in and shadow her job a couple days through the week. I pulled a few ideas from what I had learned from her and the magazines I had read and re-decorated my bedroom. Anna had liked what I had done so much that she asked me to provide a few updates in Logan's room. I pleasantly surprised Anna with what I had done, and she asked me to help her with a few things around the house.

I heard the phone ring and sat my diary aside and jumped up off my bed. I wandered down the hall to make sure everything was in place in Logan's room. I had just put the finishing touches on it yesterday and I was proud of how it had turned out. I hoped he liked it.

I was straightening the comforter on the bed when I heard the phone ring again. Surely that had to be Logan. He said he would call today and confirm his flight information so we could pick him up. I ran downstairs and went into the kitchen. Anna sat on the phone smiling at me as I entered. "No, Joe, I still haven't heard from him. Maybe I will call."

It was just my father's daily afternoon call home. I wandered over to the fridge and poured myself a glass of juice. Anna finally hung up after numerous I love you's. I couldn't get over how in love they really were and hoped that I too could have that one day.

"Have you heard from Logan?" I asked, a funny feeling kicking up in the pit of my stomach.

"No, I haven't. I'm worried, it's not like him not to have

called, but he said he would be buying his textbooks today and that he would be busy right until he came home. Are you looking forward to having him home?"

"Doesn't matter." I swallowed the last of my juice down, trying to hide my feelings and went back to the fridge for a little more. I could already feel my pulse humming with excitement over the mention of his name. Who knew what I would be like when it came time to face him.

Anna got up and began preparing the meatloaf for tonight's dinner. I was helping her by adding in the ingredients when the phone rang. "Leah, dear, could you get that please, my hands are a mess!" she said holding up her meat covered hands and wiggling her fingers at me.

"Sure thing." I laughed and reached for the handset and answered. "Hello."

"Hey." His voice, that smooth, deep voice suddenly hit me right in the stomach and I swallowed hard. "Gingersnap, is that you, I barely recognized your voice." That name still grated on everyone of my nerves, but I swore I wouldn't let him know just how much that nickname still bothered me.

"Hey, Logan." At the mention of his name Anna stopped what she was doing, quickly washed her hands and came over waiting for the phone. "Your mom is here, she is waiting to speak with you." I didn't give him a second to reply I passed her the phone.

"Hi, Logan, honey. How are you?" I could tell she missed him. She looked so happy to hear his voice and then suddenly whatever was being said on the other end of the phone wiped that smile right off her face.

"I see. So, you couldn't get the time off from work then?" she said into the phone, disappointment lacing her voice. She was quiet for a moment. "All right, well then, I guess we will see you at Thanksgiving. I will not tell you how disappointed everyone will be."

I hung my head knowing Anna had picked up things for his

favorite meal at the grocery store this week and suddenly I felt bad for her. She looked so upset and she kept holding her fingers under her nose, she always did that to hold back tears.

I stayed in the kitchen and as soon as Anna hung the phone up from speaking with Logan, I continued to help her with dinner. I didn't feel right leaving her all alone. "Are we having dessert tonight?" I asked hoping to get her to talk.

"I picked up something frozen for tonight," she mumbled mixing the breadcrumbs into the bowl of meat.

"Oh, I was looking forward to your homemade carrot cake, we haven't had it in a while. When we are finished making the meatloaf, why don't we make one. It's been a while since we baked together." She stopped mixing the meat in the bowl and looked at me, one lone tear falling from the corner of her eye.

"Leah, I would love nothing more." She wrapped one arm around me and pulled me in for a tight squeeze. I swallowed hard, fighting my own tears from falling at the news he wasn't coming home.

Once my father got home, Anna had told my father that Logan wouldn't be coming home and while I cleaned up the kitchen and got the cake in the oven both Dad and Anna went up to their room. She came back down, her eyes red from crying, and to be honest I think he was just upset as she was. We ate dinner, and I listened to my father go on about his day and after dessert I returned to my room. I flopped down onto my bed and pulled out my diary and began to write.

Dear Diary.

I'm so upset. As you know Logan was supposed to be coming home this weekend, but now he wasn't. I don't know why it's bothered me, all he ever did was pick on me, still does according to the Gingersnap comment he said tonight on the phone. I guess nothing has changed even with what happened between us. But something funny happened today when I heard his voice. My stomach flipped, and I got this funny, warm feeling inside. Maybe I'm coming down with something. Anyway, I have never seen Anna look so upset.

I dropped the pen on my diary and jumped out of bed; I had an idea. I grabbed a piece of paper and a red pen and sat down at my desk. I would write him a letter and tell him exactly what he was missing by not coming home. With the paper in front of me I thought for a couple of moments. I decided I would talk to him about Labor Day since this was the first holiday he would miss with us.

Dear Logan,

It's Labor Day! I cannot tell you how much fun we are having without you here, but I will try. We went down to the waterfront tonight and the minute those fireworks went off; it was as if the entire city was celebrating your absence. Oh, and just for you, I ate a hot dog; you know how much I hate those! We also had brownie sundaes in your honor, made from your favorite brownie cake. Do you want to know the best part: I didn't have to share any of it with you. We even had whipped cream, chocolate and caramel sauce, all that we could eat. Hope Boston is as hot and humid as the weatherman was predicting, guess you should start preparing for hell now.

Leah

I giggled at the last part. I folded the letter and placed it into an envelope and addressed it to Logan's school address and the next morning I mailed it.

Weeks had gone by. I had finally given up checking the mail every day when I got home. There had been no response from Logan. I had started back to school and had buried myself in school work. It was getting close to Christmas, and I was in my room filling out college applications when Anna came to my door.

"Leah, we are going to go and get the tree now. Are you

coming?" I looked up from the paperwork I was filling in and smiled.

"Oh yeah, give me two minutes, I'll be right down." I quickly finished what I was working on and grabbed my sweater and cell phone from the end of the bed. I needed a picture of us tonight, I wanted to make sure that Logan could see what a great time we were having without him. I planned to give him his letter at Christmas while he was home. After all, I couldn't stop now, I had already sent him three more letters since Labor Day.

On Veteran's Day, yes, Veteran's Day, it doesn't matter how minute the holiday was; I planned to send him one for every holiday. On Veteran's Day, I told him we were having a fabulous time down at the waterfront ceremony and how it was too bad he would never have the chance to be honored since he wasn't in the military. On Halloween, I took a photo of the three of us out front the house handing out candy and told him not to bother buying himself another mask as his face was already scary enough. Oh, and on Thanksgiving, I included a family photo of the three of us and told him his absence was what I was most thankful for this year. Was it mean, sure, but this had become a fun little game I wasn't ready to give up, yet.

Dad, Anna and I walked through the Christmas tree lot together, hot chocolate in hand, looking for our perfect tree. "What about this one?" I asked taking a sip of my steaming cup.

"Jeez, Leah, it's a little large," Dad said holding his hand above his head to give it a measure. "It's over eight feet tall there is no way it will fit in the living room." I giggled, I always wanted these huge trees from the time I was little, and Dad knew it.

"I think this one would be perfect," Anna sang out pointing to one across the way, poking me on the shoulder while nodding and smiling in the direction she had sent my dad.

My father did the same thing, held his hand up to measure its height. "Now I have two of you to compete with."

We both laughed and took another sip of our hot chocolate

continuing to look for our tree. Another half an hour and we had found the perfect tree. Before the guy wrapped it up, I asked Anna and Dad to pose with me in front of it. We all held up our hot chocolate and smiled for the picture. It was the perfect one to include in Logan's Christmas letter.

As soon as we got home, I went back up to my room and grabbed a piece of paper. I quickly threw in a sheet of photo paper and printed the photo I took before I grabbed a green pen and started my letter.

Dear Logan,

We had a great time tonight picking out the tree. You would have loved the hot chocolate, it contained your favorite little marsh-mallows, so I had the lady put extra in mine since you weren't there. I guess you could say I had yours too. Too bad you gave up chocolate, you'll never get to taste that combo again. Oh, and know that I am enjoying drinking all your mother's eggnog and not having to share it with you this year. And just so you know, I came up with the perfect resolution for New Years, to forget that you ever existed!

Leah

Christmas came and went without Logan. He said he couldn't possibly make the trip home between semesters because of his job and the amount of studying he had to do to be prepared for classes to start up after the first of the year. It was just too much to take the time off. So, once again, I got to watch as he broke Anna's heart, and while she cried on my father's shoulder, I fought back the tears that were threatening to pour down my cheeks. On Christmas Day, Anna spent most of her time in the kitchen keeping herself busy. New Years was the same, it too came and went without Logan.

Over time, I never stopped thinking of Logan or writing to him every holiday. I soon discovered that not only did I miss him but the reason I had convinced myself that I hated him so much was because my crush on him had never really ended. I missed those blue eyes, the way he wore his baseball cap back-wards, the smell of his cologne and the truth was that kiss we had shared haunted my every waking moment. I never called him, I would just bide my time until the next holiday came around and write to him then. I soon started including little gifts with my letters, all things I knew he hated. I think the best one had to be the black licorice I included with his Valentine's Day letter.

No responses ever came, even the few times I spoke with him when he called, he never mentioned them. As the years continued to pass, Logan never returned home—though Anna and Daddy went to Boston for a few visits over the years—and his calls became few and far between. I figured he probably had found himself a girlfriend and was now too busy to even read my letters since he was too busy to call his mother on a weekly basis.

I lifted my case into my trunk and slammed it shut. Another consultation in the books. I was feeling defeated, everything I did for this firm was the same, there was never any challenge, nothing exciting or new. I had graduated the top of my class, and I was damn good at what I did, and I wanted a challenge, I didn't want to spend the next twenty-five years redesigning Martha's living room. I wanted to design grand hotels, and office buildings and account executives' homes. I climbed into the front seat and started my car. I was about to turn on the radio when my cell phone pinged. I grabbed it and looked at the notifications—it had been going off all during the meeting. I had three emails from work letting me know of my three newly booked appointments, doing the same old mundane things. God, I hated this town, nothing changed. I closed my eyes for a moment resting my head back on the headrest. Why hadn't I heard anything from the companies I had applied to last week? There couldn't be that many interior designers out there vying for positions.

I threw my phone down on the console and went to pull away from the curb when it rang. I glanced down at the number —out of the area. I frowned, perhaps it was Jenna, "Hello," I said into the mouthpiece.

"Hi, could I speak with Leah Tate, please."

"You've got her."

"Hi, Leah, my name is Mary. I'm calling from Preston Interior Design in Boston. Your resume crossed my desk yesterday and I'm very impressed." My jaw dropped, I was suddenly glad I wasn't driving for fear I would have crashed my brand-new car, "Leah, I would like to set up an interview. I wasn't looking for a designer, but I will make an exception. Now I understand you would have to travel so I think Skype would work just fine."

I swallowed hard, this design firm was exactly what I wanted and the fact they called me without even looking for a designer was unbelievable. "Absolutely."

"How does your schedule look tomorrow at two?"

I glanced down at my day planner that always sat open on my passenger seat. I was scheduled to meet with Mr. and Mrs. Simpson to discuss the redesign their living room and kitchen. "I'm available." I would worry about the Simpsons later.

"Perfect. I will speak with you then."

"Thank you, Mary, I look forward to it."

As I drove home, I felt lighter than I had in months, and if this went well, I could finally get out of this mundane little town and leave behind everything. I wanted to start my life over and maybe meet someone instead of holding onto a hope and dream that would never come true.

By the time I arrived home, Anna and Dad had gone out for dinner with a couple of friends. I changed into my yoga pants and a t-shirt, threw a frozen pizza into the oven and pulled out my anniversary party planner. I was planning a surprise ten-year party for them. After all, neither of them made it to ten years in their previous marriages. Dad and Mom had divorced after six years, and Anna's husband had died. Tonight, I needed to send out the invites online. I sat at the kitchen table eating pizza and drinking a soda and made my list of invitees. Then I grabbed my laptop from my bag and went straight to Facebook. I planned to make the party event there but first I wandered to Logan's profile and looked through his pictures. He had uploaded a more recent picture—as handsome as ever now, he wore his hair shorter and looked as if he kept a little scruff on his chiseled face. His blue eyes still danced like they always had, and it looked like he was still working out. I opened the little messenger chat box and wrote him a message to invite him personally but stopped. I would send him an invitation just like everyone else but because we had almost no communication since he had left for college, I felt silly messaging him directly.

I had even stopped sending him holiday letters after Christmas. It felt odd not sending one now because Valentine's Day was just around the corner, but I needed to move on. Ten years was a long time.

I shut his profile down and created the event for the anniversary party. Somewhere deep inside of me I was secretly hoping that Logan would come, his mom missed him so much, I thought it would be amazing to see her face light up at seeing him. I too missed him.

It surprised me to hear her talking to my father one night about Logan. He apparently still wasn't dating anyone and that worried her, but my father assured her he probably just hadn't found the one yet.

After I had sent the invites, I called the Simpsons and moved their appointment from two to four, making something up as the reason for the reschedule. Then I spent the rest of the night learning more about Preston Interior Design. I wanted this job more than anything, this opportunity was just what I needed.

❧

"I got the job!" I sang as I walked through the front door, two weeks later. I had been sitting in the coffee shop on my lunch break when I got the call. I could barely contain my excitement and thought about taking the rest of the day off after I had heard the news. Instead, after I calmed down, I had returned to work and handed in my notice. I felt it only fair to give them more than the standard two weeks after being there for five years.

Anna came out from the kitchen and smiled. "I knew it, I just knew you would get it. Congratulations, Leah. When do you start?" she asked leaning against the armchair holding a towel in her hand.

"Right after your anniversary, so three weeks."

"Your father will be so proud of you, but don't be like my son and decide not to come back and visit us. I can't handle losing you both." I hugged her then I sat my things on the floor while I took my coat off and hung it in the closet.

"Anna, I wouldn't dream of not coming back home and miss all those wonderful deserts you bake."

"Speaking of which I will whip something up, this is cause for a celebration." She ran off into the kitchen and started banging bowls around. I smiled since Anna would look for any reason to bake something sinfully delicious.

I ran up to my room to get changed. I checked my laptop first for more responses. I had sent the invitations out two weeks ago and almost everyone had responded except for Logan. As I logged in, I silently prayed he had responded, the excitement growing in the pit of my stomach as the page loaded. Once again, I was disappointed to see that his name still hadn't moved from the invitee list. I tapped my fingers on the desktop debating sending him a text but decided against it. I needed to let him go; this wasn't healthy. I shut the laptop and quickly changed from my work clothes into my sweats and took my makeup off.

10
Logan

I glanced at the clock on the wall and went back to studying the plans in front of me. I could finally work on my own stuff now that the firm had closed for the day. I was living in the same bachelor pad I had gotten after my last year of school all those years ago and would until my house was finally built. They had already poured the foundation, and we were getting ready to frame this week. I had designed the whole concept and couldn't wait to see it come to life. My dream was finally coming true, building the perfect home to support the perfect family. In three months, I would live in my dream home, albeit alone, because I still hadn't found the perfect woman, one I would be happy to call mine, but still I was halfway there.

"Hey, Logan, you about ready to go?" John asked stopping at my office door.

"Yep, whenever you are." John was my neighbor, co-worker and best friend. We carpooled to work every day and spent weekends together cruising around Boston and hanging at local clubs. Although now he was seeing Cynthia our nights out were few. I rolled up my plans and shoved them back into the tube. I grabbed my briefcase and the plans I needed to work on tonight and made my way down to John's office. I spent most nights working at home and being it was Valentine's Day today I already knew I wouldn't be going anywhere tonight.

We walked into the apartment building lobby together and I went straight to my mailbox. I couldn't wait to see what Leah had cooked up for me this year. She had written me a letter every single holiday, never missing one, no matter how insignificant, since I had moved out. I had grown so used to receiving them and looked forward to them. I opened the little mailbox, my heart racing in anticipation when I saw the stack of mail waiting for me. "You waiting for something? You've been talking about the mail all day." John laughed. He was right, I had been talking about it all day, because I couldn't wait to see what she had sent, her perfect handwriting, her words, I guess you could almost call me obsessed.

"Yeah, you could say that," I said routing through the pile of mail that had been roughly shoved inside the mail cubby. I flipped through the bills and flyers, my heartbeat speeding up as I was coming near the end of the pile.

"You have a girlfriend I don't know about, or perhaps one of those sexy pen-pals from overseas. If that's the case, I want to see a picture." John let out a laugh.

"No, no, nothing like that," I said frowning as I reached the end of the pile and started my search through the bundle all over again in case I had missed the pink paper she always sent for Valentine's Day, but the second search revealed exactly what the first had—nothing. All there was were bills and junk mail. "It's not here," I mumbled more to myself.

"What's not there?" John asked, now pulling out his own mail.

"Just a letter I've been waiting for." I shoved the mail into my briefcase, disappointed, and pressed the button for the elevator. As I stood there waiting, I couldn't tear my mind from that damn letter. It should be here, I mean I hadn't gotten my mail in a week and over the years, Leah had gotten damn good at getting those letters to arrive on the actual holiday, not a day before or after. "It is the fourteenth, right?" I asked John who now stood beside me.

"All day, man, all day. Which reminds me I forgot fucking roses. I've got to run and get those. If you see Cynthia, just let her know I had to run back to the office, okay."

"Sure thing." I watched as he ran out the door, in some ways I was glad I didn't have to deal with that yet.

Once I had gotten changed, I heated leftovers from the night before and ate dinner in front of the TV, just like I always did. I flipped through the channels trying to clear my mind but the fact the letter hadn't arrived was bothering me more than it should have. I even ran back down and double checked that I hadn't missed it because it was pushed up against the wall of the mailbox, but there was nothing.

I slammed my apartment door and went straight to the closet. I reached up to the top shelf and pulled out the little shoe box that sat there. I took it to the couch and removed the lid. Inside sat nine year's worth of letters mixed with funny odd little gifts. I pulled out the one that stuck out most and opened the pink envelope.

Logan,

Happy Valentine's Day! Hope you enjoy this black licorice, black instead of red because it matches the color of your heart!

Leah

I smiled as I dug through the box and found the disgusting black licorice buried in the bottom and flipped the box over in my hand. I continued routing through reading and re-reading all the letters she had sent me over the years. I remembered receiving every single one of them and although I never answered her, for reasons only I knew, I was utterly gutted that one hadn't arrived today. This was the first holiday in ten years she hadn't sent me anything, I guess perhaps some guy had won her heart and she had forgotten about me. The thought piqued my curiosity, who would Gingersnap date, she was so pouty and bratty most of the time. The only thing I knew had changed about her was her language in her letters, it had become more sophisticated over the years, I silently wondered if maybe the rest of her had caught up. I grabbed my cell phone and opened Facebook.

The only notification I had was an invitation from Leah to

my parents ten-year wedding anniversary. I glanced through the photos she had posted. I hadn't seen my mother in a few years; she looked great, almost as if she had aged in reverse. The anniversary party was being held in two weeks. I quickly glanced at my calendar, that is the weekend they were supposed to close in the framing on my house. I knew John would probably look after all that for me, it would only be one weekend.

Without giving it a second thought, I quickly booked a ticket to head back home for the party. I thought about responding to the invite but decided I would let it be a surprise, not only for my mother, but for Leah as well. I wanted my damn Valentine's Day letter, and I would get it, even if it meant going back home.

11
Logan

I woke and looked around the room through blurry vision, almost forgetting where I was. I stared at a chair I didn't recognize and then I remembered that I had taken the red eye in last night so I wouldn't have to miss a day of work. I was swamped with projects and couldn't afford any extra time off. I ran my hand over my face and reached for the room service menu that sat on my bedside table. I was starving and tired since I had only had two hours of sleep. I had thought about going to see everyone this morning for breakfast but decided last night it may be better to wait and see Mom alone after everyone had left for the day.

I read through the menu, pancakes and bacon catching my eye. I picked up the phone and placed an order then I jumped into the shower while I was waiting. A long shower was just what I needed and after thirty minutes of letting the hot water run over my aching body, I shut the water off and wrapped the white towel around my waist. As soon as I stepped out of the bathroom, I could smell the fresh blueberry pancakes and found them under a covered plate on the desk. I poured a cup of coffee from the little coffee maker and sat down at the desk and dug into the stack of steaming pancakes after dousing them in syrup.

I drank down my cup of coffee, refilling it after I finished eating and then headed into the bathroom to shave. I normally kept my beard trimmed short, but I had been working so much I had little time to worry about it, but I didn't want to see my mother without looking half decent.

It was close to ten thirty by the time I had finally gotten dressed. I grabbed my wallet and keys and headed out the door. I figured Mom should be alone by now, everyone else would be working. I had a good half hour drive to the house. As I drove down the once familiar streets of the old neighborhood, it was like time had stood still in this small town.

I finally pulled into the driveway the house looked the same as it had the day I left. I turned down the music and sat there for a moment. I had vowed never to return home after I left for Boston, and I had succeeded, until now. I didn't even know what I was doing here. I didn't know how I would face Leah after that kiss we had shared, and how I ran after wards. I got cold feet and was about to back out of the driveway when I caught a movement in the front window. My mom stood there looking out at the unfamiliar car that was sitting in the driveway, my car. As I watched her through the window, I shut the car off and climb out, taking my time to walk to the front door. I had opened the screen door and was just about to knock when the door was pulled open and my mother stood in front of me with tears in her eyes.

"Logan, is it really you?"

"Yeah, Mom, it's me."

She wrapped her arms around me and pulled me in for a tight hug. "My god, it's so good to see you. My little man all grown up, looking as handsome as his father."

I pulled out of her embrace and looked at her, really looked at her. She didn't have that exhausted look she used to have, nor the deep dark circles under her eyes. She wore black dress pants and an expensive white sweater, her hair professionally colored and styled, she even wore makeup. I couldn't remember a time I had seen her wear makeup. She was well looked after, about ten pounds lighter and she carried a sense of peace and happiness about her.

"You look great, Mom. I'm glad to see you're taking care of yourself."

"Thanks, honey. It's easy to do it when you have the money and time and aren't run off your feet every waking second. Come in, are you here for the party? Leah didn't tell me you were coming."

I stepped inside the house and noticed it had been redesigned by a professional, everything had its place. "That's because she doesn't know, I didn't respond to the invite. I wanted it to be a surprise," I said continuing to take everything in. "How do you know about the party, the invite said it was a surprise?"

"Well, Leah had to tell us, we were planning to go away for the weekend." She smiled. "And yes, I'm surprised. Joe will be so happy to see you. Come in, tell me what is new? Where are you working? Are you dating anyone?"

I removed my shoes and together we sat down. You would almost think I didn't speak to my mother on the phone by the way she was acting. "No, Mom, I'm not dating anyone. I'm in the middle of building my dream home though. Maybe after that is done, I will find someone to share my life with, if not no big deal. Did you want to see it?" I pulled my phone from my pocket and showed her the pictures of what they had accomplished and then I pulled up the floor plan.

"You designed this?" she asked studying the plans. "Maybe I should talk to Joe about hiring you to design us our dream retirement home. He promises he is getting ready to retire sometime soon." She giggled.

"I did, Mom, I designed it. I would be happy to do something for you guys. I mean you guys paid for my education."

"So where are you staying? You're more than welcome to stay here, your old room has been waiting for you?"

"Thanks." I didn't have the heart to tell her that I was staying at the hotel by the airport.

"Let me grab you a coffee," she said getting up from the couch and heading into the kitchen. I looked around the room, "You've done great things in here, Mom." I heard her banging in the kitchen, finally returning with a tray holding two mugs of hot coffee, and a piece of her chocolate cake for me.

"Here you go," she said handing me my mug and the slice of cake. I dug the fork into the soft moist cake, it tasted like it always had. "Leah did all the work on the house, she's an interior designer now."

I looked around the room, everything flowed together well. I swallowed hard, "Wow, she did a great job."

"You think you can get along for the weekend?"

"Who knows, depends on her." I shrugged, my normal attitude when it came to her coming through.

"Logan, don't be ridiculous, you are both adults now."

I was dying to ask her where she was, if she still lived here, how she was doing, who she was dating or married to, but I couldn't give myself away. If my mother thought for a second that I cared, she would wonder what was going on. I didn't need her to be suspicious. I left the topic of Leah alone and soon we were wrapped up in conversation and we passed the afternoon away talking and getting reacquainted. It had been so long since I had seen my mom, and it was nice to just spend the time talking with her. I missed her a lot. I had been so wrong before I left, and I felt the need to apologize to her, Joe had looked after Mom just the way she had said he would. I had been foolish to think otherwise.

Shortly before dinner Mom had to run out to the store to grab a couple things for the dish she planned to make. She had offered to take me with her but with the time difference and all the travel I was tired, so I decided to just stay and hang out until she got back. I put the magazine down I had been reading and wandered into the kitchen. A sense of déjà vu came over me as I grabbed a glass and opened the fridge looking for juice. I poured the cold orange liquid into the glass and shut the door and that was when my eyes caught her beautiful red hair. I stared for a moment, taking her in, and then I let my eyes wash slowly over the rest of her, it was like I was on sensory overload. The outfit she wore accentuated her soft curves, I wanted to run my hands over them, and my mouth nearly watered at the sight of her lips. She stood leaning up against the door frame her arms crossed in front of her. "What are you doing here?" she asked, a smirk playing on the corner of her mouth.

I could barely take my eyes off her, she had grown up, and the way her green eyes danced over my body told me she was as happy to see me as I was her, or so I hoped. "Well, someone didn't send me my usual Valentine's Day letter, so I came to get it in person."

"Don't hold your breath, Logan, there is no letter." She walked over and took the juice out of my hand and brought the glass to her lips. I stared at those perfect kissable lips, the ones I had dreamed of kissing for the past ten years. She never took her eyes from mine as she drank the cold liquid. "You know I never loved you."

She placed the cold glass back in my hand. I watched her eyes do another quick sweep of my body, then she turned and looked over her shoulder at me, smiling, before heading upstairs. I firmly planted my eyes on her tight ass as she walked away from me. I wanted so bad to grab it and pin her against the wall and do things to her that I shouldn't even be thinking about doing. Instead, I quickly averted my thoughts and my eyes when I heard the front door slam and my mother came into the kitchen carrying a bag full of groceries.

"Logan, what on earth is wrong?" she asked looking at me.

"What do you mean?" I asked as I took a sip of the orange juice, still imagining Leah's kissable lips on mine.

"You look like you did when you were ten years old, as if you were doing something you shouldn't be." She laughed.

Just thinking of fucking my stepsister ten ways to Sunday, I thought to myself. I finished my juice and then helped Mom put the groceries away.

I stood in my room leaning up against the cold wooden door. Every part of my body was on fire after that encounter, with need and anger. How dare he show up. I had sent that invite weeks ago and suddenly here he was, in the kitchen. I hadn't known how to react when I saw him. The first thing that had gone through my mind was how badly I wanted to feel his lips and hands on me, everywhere. I had never gotten the sight of naked Logan out of my mind after that night in the hallway. I wanted him then, and apparently still wanted him now. However, I had to hide those thoughts quickly, especially when he brought up that damn letter. I didn't think he even bothered reading them, but apparently, I had been wrong.

I had finally calmed down and now I stood in the kitchen putting the finishing touches on the desert I had made, while Logan, Anna, and my father were talking in the other room. They were laughing and joking with Logan while he told them all about the projects he was working on. I listened from the kitchen; it sounded like he had become very successful, working for a large architectural firm in downtown Boston. I was happy for him, he deserved it. I had overheard him mention something about building his home in one of the more scenic areas of Boston.

"Are you seeing anyone?" I heard Dad ask him as I put a couple more strawberries on the top of the chocolate cake I had made. I listened harder than I should have, and I prayed that he was still single, "Will there be wedding bells anytime soon?" I held my breath as I waited for him to answer.

Logan cleared his throat. "No, sir, I'll have the perfect house for the perfect family, but no one special to share it with." As I heard his words, I released the breath, I was holding. A sense of peace came over me at hearing his answer. I shouldn't care, but I did, I cared a lot.

"Oh, sweetie, you will? Look at how happy Joe and I are. It takes time. Honestly, I figured you would be settled down by now, maybe with a little one on the way."

"Oh god, Mom. I've dated, but no one holds my attention long enough. I want the perfect picture, and I'm not willing to settle. So, until that time, I will have a beautiful home and my dream job. The rest will come when it comes. And nothing you're going to say will make me hurry and change my mind." He let out a laugh.

I heard my dad laugh too. "Logan, I won't tell you the picture doesn't exist, because look what I now have, but I will tell you it took me years to find it. Don't waste your youth. Have fun."

Logan let out a laugh. "Believe me, I'm not wasting my youth. I want the perfect family and I will not settle for anything less."

My heart sunk a little at his response, "I'm not wasting." I wondered what type of woman he dated, how many women he had slept with.

"Anna, your son is as stubborn as you."

I giggled at what my father had said, Logan was stubborn, I was glad I wasn't the only one who saw it. I grabbed the head of lettuce and was just about to prepare the salad when I felt a large warm hand on my waist and felt someone close behind me.

"You aren't going to poison me, are you?" I felt the light puff of his breath on my neck as I heard his deep sexy voice ask me, his cologne invaded my senses.

"I thought about it, but I'll let you live, at least for this visit,"

I said turning, looking into those blue eyes. The anxious feeling that ran through me from his touch made my voice quiver.

"So, Mom tells me you are an interior designer," he said pulling away from me and leaning against the counter opposite of me.

"Yep. I work for a small company here, it's not exactly what I wanted, but it pays the bills." I had only told my father and Anna that I would be moving and had asked that they not say anything to anyone else until I had announced it. At this point I would announce it on Saturday since I had to leave the following week, but I wouldn't announce where I was moving, at least, not with Logan present, I would tell others afterwards.

"My god, they've been alone in the same room for fifteen minutes and they haven't killed one another yet," I heard Anna say behind us.

"It's about time, after all they are adults. Logan, come sit with me. Tell me more about what you do while the girls get dinner." Logan looked at me and smiled and went and sat down beside my father and they continued chatting about his life back in Boston.

Anna pulled the roast from the oven while I continued with the salad and vegetables. As Logan sat talking to my father, I couldn't take my eyes off him. The longest I hadn't looked at him was when he was in the living room and I was in the kitchen and I had still found reasons to go into the other room while he talked to Anna and Dad. He had grown up; he was always good-looking but now he was gorgeous. After he had left for school, I had dated several guys and subconsciously all I did was compare them to Logan. At first, I hadn't even realized I had been doing it until I was sitting having coffee with Jenna one afternoon.

"You realize that since he has left his name hasn't left your lips right," she had said one afternoon. I almost choked on my hot chocolate. "Seriously, Leah, you're always telling me some-thing, Logan got an award, they voted him MVP of the football team. Logan called the other night. He is all you talk about."

I went home that night and looked through my diary, every entry for the past six months had been about Logan since the night he kissed me in the kitchen. That was when it had dawned on me, not only had I been crushing on him in high school, I was still crushing on him after we moved into this house. It had just gotten worse after that kiss. I had already started with the letters and I kept them going, counting down the days between every holiday waiting to send them to him. Eventually I had even stopped dating and buried myself in school work.

I thought back to those letters, the only reason for them was to get him to answer me, acknowledge me. Instead, what I had done was pour myself into each one, finding some way to insult him in every letter so not to give my true feelings away, when all I probably had to do was stop writing them and he would return.

"Leah, dear, would you help me serve up dinner?" Anna asked now plating the roast.

Joe and Logan both continued sitting and talking while I pulled out more serving dishes. As soon as I was away from Anna and in the opposite corner, I couldn't help but glance over at the table. I couldn't help checking him out, those eyes and lips, the smooth skin of his neck that lead to his broad shoulders and chest. "It's nice to have him home," Anna whispered interrupting my thoughts and startling me, while handing over a bowl of carrots. I recovered easily and smiled gently, taking the bowl from her. "He seems happy."

Once again, I glanced over at the table, this time locking eyes with him, his blue eyes sparkling. As I carried the bowl over to the table, I watched as his eyes washed over my body in a way a brother shouldn't look at his sister. I could still feel his eyes on me as I walked back over to Anna to grab more dishes.

"Anna, did he show you the floor plan to his house?" Dad asked while Anna helped bring the remaining dishes to the table. I took my seat across from Logan and dished out food onto my plate.

"Yes, he did. I wanted to talk about that with you," she said as she sat down and passed a bowl of potatoes to Logan. "I thought perhaps we could have him design us a home, for our retirement."

"I like that idea."

As Dad and Anna were talking, I kept my head down sliding my fork around my plate, Logan's words from earlier playing through my mind, "I came to get my letter." I looked up and saw he was watching me from across the table, a sly smile on his lips. Then suddenly I felt his foot run up the side of my leg.

I jumped up from the table. "Anyone want more iced tea?" I choked out grabbing my glass from the table.

My father looked at me and then to my glass, "Leah, what is the matter with you, your glass is still full."

"Yeah but . . ."

"No buts, Leah, now sit down."

I looked over at Logan who sat there with a shit-eating grin on his face, just like he used to do when we were younger, but that was over picking on me, not running his foot up my leg. I slowly sat back down, the conversation soon returning to normal. The only thing not normal was that for the rest of the dinner my stepbrother sat across from me, eyeing me, and playing footsie with me under the table.

"Dessert was fantastic, Mom," Logan said dropping his fork on his plate and picking up his mug of coffee.

"Oh, no, don't thank me, dessert was all Leah." He looked over and then swiped his finger through the chocolate icing still on the plate and sucked the icing off his finger while looking me directly in the eyes. All that ran through my mind was his tongue licking chocolate icing from my body. I could feel heat rise to my cheeks as I studied the look on his face.

He glanced at his watch and let out a large yawn. "This damn time difference is a killer."

"You're more than welcome to stay in your old room," Anna said rounding up the dessert dishes.

I almost dropped my coffee at her suggestion. He couldn't stay in this house with me across the hall. I looked up and met Logan's eyes, but I knew what was written on my face and it was nothing but a plea, begging for him to stay. The rational part of my brain saying no, the slut in me saying yes. "No, Mom, I'm staying at the Hilton, near the airport off McGill Road. room three sixty-eight." I hung onto his every word permanently storing that information in my mind.

"Oh, honey, it's such a far drive, are you sure you won't just stay?"

He didn't answer right away, instead he looked at me, studying my face. "Yep, I'm sure. I guess I will see you all on Saturday!" He gently smiled at them before turning his eyes to me, then he stood from the table and grabbed his jacket. He nodded at me. Dad and Anna followed him to the front door and said goodnight where they waited until he had driven away.

I was still sitting in my chair in the kitchen, fiddling with my phone, and drinking my coffee when my father and Anna returned to the kitchen. "Leah, help Anna with the dishes, please." I ignored what he said. All that was running through my mind was Logan's room number. I had a nagging feeling in my gut that I needed to see him, to clear the air once and for all over that damn kiss.

"Leah, did you hear what I said."

I put my phone into my pocket, "Sorry, Anna, Dad, I have to go to the office. I got an email regarding a client."

"Leah, it's eight thirty?" my father said. "And tomorrow is your day off."

"I know but it's important, Dad." I stood and kissed them both on the cheek then I grabbed my coat and purse from the hall closet and made my way out the front door to my car.

As soon as I got into the car, I leaned my head back against the headrest allowing my heart to calm down. It was rapidly beating in my chest as I pulled the seatbelt across me and plugged it into the lock. The loud click reverberating in my ears.

He wanted a damn Valentine's Day letter; he would get one. I could feel the anger boiling in me, leaving me without saying goodbye after kissing me like he had. I had ten fucking years of buildup to get rid of. I started the engine and slammed the car into reverse pulling out of the driveway and speeding off before I lost my nerve.

13
Logan

I opened the door, flipped the lights on and walked into my empty hotel room. My pulse hadn't stopped racing since I had seen her behind the fridge door. I struggled to keep my eyes off her, which was hard since I spent most of my time talking with her father as she sat in the background. She had grown into a remarkable woman, both smart and attractive even though she still infuriated me.

I toed my shoes off and lay down on the bed, letting out a breath. I grabbed the remote and flipped the TV on, then pulled my shirt off and threw it down on top of my gym bag. I ran my hands over my face as I wondered if she would come to me, there was no other reason to drop the address and room number to the whole family.

I was just about asleep when someone knocked on the door. I prayed that she stood on the other side of it. Although who did I think I was kidding, she still hated me and the very air I breathed. I climbed off the bed, walked over to door and pulled it open. My heart skipped a beat as soon as I caught a glimpse of that long red hair. She stood with her back to the door looking down the hallway. My eyes traveled down to her round delectable ass. I cleared my throat, and she quickly turned, a look of surprise on her face. I followed her eyes down my chest to the open button on my jeans. Her cheeks grew red as she stood there, and I couldn't help but watch as her tongue darted out of her mouth wetting her lips. "Well, are you going to ask me in or are you going to be rude and leave me out here in the hall?"

I stepped to the side and waved my arm for her to come in. She removed her coat as she walked through the door and threw it on the chair along with her purse.

"So, you finally return home after all this time. Come back and be the perfect son."

"What's your problem, Gingersnap? Jealous?"

She let out a little laugh. "No, Logan, I'm not jealous. It's just you waltzed back in here like you haven't been gone for ten years and expected everything to be the same. What is it you want?"

"I want nothing, well no, that's not true, I told you what I came back for." I smirked, pushing the door closed. I followed her into the room and leaned against the little desk.

"You don't honestly expect me to believe you traveled halfway across the country to get some stupid Valentine's Day letter from me, do you?"

"Yes, why wouldn't I. You were the one who wrote all those years, and just suddenly stopped? So yes, I was curious why you stopped, and I want my letter."

"Logan don't play it up like any of them ever mattered, because I know for a fact they didn't. If they had, you would have written back or called, something."

"I've called," I said holding my hands up.

"Yes, to speak to your mother. You never called me after you left, you didn't even make the time to say goodbye."

"As if it would have mattered?"

I was quiet, he really thought it didn't matter? Only I wasn't talking about him not saying goodbye. I was talking about the two unforgettable kisses we had shared. I swallowed hard, "Yes, it mattered. Did it not matter to you?"

He looked around the room and then ran his hand over his face, closing his eyes. "Really, are you blind, Gingersnap? Do you really have to ask me that? Have you not seen the way I have been staring at you all night? Did you not see the way I was looking at you before I left for school?"

She swallowed hard and looked me in the eye. I could tell she didn't know what to say.

"I've seen the way your body reacts every time we touch, even before I left. That night in the kitchen, your body tensed at the feel of my lips on yours and I thought you might be stiff for weeks. I haven't forgotten the way your eyes looked at me as the towel lay on the floor of the hallway, I wanted you so fucking bad, but you ran. I didn't think you'd want to hear from me, but I remember, Gingersnap, I remember it all.

"Tonight, I spent half the night flirting with you and the other half running my foot over yours, right in front of our parents. Don't think for one second, I couldn't see the way your pulse sped up. The way your skin flushed, pupils dilated, even the way your breathing changed, and this little spot right here," I said reaching out and brushing my fingers across the soft skin of her neck, "This spot gives you away every time you get excited or embarrassed. That is how I always knew if I were getting to you." He stepped closer and whispered, "And just so you know, those 'stupid cards' as you call them, they mattered more than you will ever know."

I felt my body tingle as I finished dragging my fingers across her soft skin. I knew I couldn't hold back much longer; I could already feel the pain building from my cock being so hard. Her eyes traveled my body before making their way back up to my eyes, then I watched as she licked her lips.

I stared at her, watching her, taking her in. For some reason I felt I needed to prove to her just how much those letters mattered. "Dear Logan, we had a great time tonight picking out the tree. You would have loved the hot chocolate, it contained your favorite little marshmallows, so I had the lady put extra in mine since you weren't there. I guess you could say I had yours too. Too bad you gave up chocolate, you'll never get to taste that combo again. Oh, and know that I am enjoying drinking all your mother's eggnog and not having to share it with you this year. And just so you know, I came up with the perfect resolution for New Years, to forget that you ever existed! Love Leah. I received that letter the year I moved out." Her mouth fell open as she realized that I had memorized her words.

"You memorized my letters?" she asked shocked. I didn't give her a chance to say anything else or to fight with me, instead I pushed her against the wall and took her mouth hungrily. Ten years of restraint had built up to this moment and now that she was within arms reach, I had to take her. I was prepared for a slap, or to be shoved away but she surprised me by wrapping her arms around my neck and kissing me back.

I wrapped my arm around her while my other hand fiddled with the buttons on her blouse, opening each one until I felt her warm skin against mine. A moment later, I undid the button of her jeans, reaching my hand down and running my fingers over her silk panties, she was already wet, and I felt my body shudder at the thought of sliding into her. She shrugged out of her shirt letting it fall to the floor and wrapped her arms around me tighter.

I walked our intertwined bodies until the back of her knees hit the mattress and she fell back against the mattress. She looked up at me as I bent over her and took her mouth, kissing her again a little slower this time, while my hands explored her body. Her nipples were hard as I cupped her breasts, running my thumbs over them. I continued, sliding my hands down to her jeans and I inched both her jeans and panties down her body. Kneeling on the edge of the bed, I kissed the insides of her knees, making my way up her thighs, as I quickly slid out of my pants.

"You have protection?" she whispered in my ear and looked up at me. I reached for my wallet that laid on the table beside the bed and pulled out the only condom I had. Thank god I had made the time to run back up to my apartment to get it.

"You don't seriously keep a condom in your wallet, do you?"

she said giggling, "Oh my god." She ran her hands over her face, shaking her head.

I gave her a look, but she kept giggling as I tore the package open with my teeth. As I slid the condom over me, I glanced at her, she was watching me, a devilish look in her eyes.

"Didn't you ever take sex ed? You broke two rules!"

I looked at her and smiled but I said nothing. I'd broken two rules, but I was also about to break three, the third being my rule, never ever to touch her.

I pushed my forearms under her knees and pulled her closer. "Ready," I whispered running my cock over her clit, she let out a moan that I felt to my very core. After checking once more to make sure she was ready for me, I positioned myself at her opening and slid into her, going slow so she could feel every single inch of me. She let out a gorgeous moan and cocked her head back. I ran my tongue over her nipple as I thrust into her again harder than before. I ran the pad of my thumb over her clit repeatedly as I continued to thrust deeply into her, her nails raking across my back.

With every pump I went deeper, and she moaned louder, and every time my thumb stroked her clit the wetter she became. She felt fucking amazing. "You going to cum for me, baby?" I whispered in her ear.

"Logan, don't stop," she panted, as I felt her tighten around me. I could feel a rush of warmth as she let herself go, seconds later I poured myself into her.

The smell of coffee roused me from my sleep. I opened my eyes and looked around the unfamiliar room trying to remember where I was. Rolling over, the intense ache I felt between my legs reminded me where I was, and then the memories of last night all came rushing back. We had spent the night fucking each other's brains out and after that we shared a pizza and a couple of beers before two more intense rounds, and then we fell asleep wrapped in one another's arms.

My clothes had already been neatly folded and were laying at the bottom of the bed. Logan's were stuffed inside his bag that sat across the room in the chair. I knew for a fact they hadn't been left like that last night. I looked to the side table, a glass of orange juice and a croissant sat next to me. I glanced at the clock noting it was only seven forty-five.

I felt the bed move and looked down to the end, Logan sat there fully dressed putting on his shoes. With the sheet wrapped securely around my upper body, I sat forward and wrapped my arms around him, hugging him. "Good morning," I said breathing in his scent and kissing him on the cheek.

He jumped up from where he had been sitting and grabbed his coat off the bed. Something was wrong, I could feel it. "Where are you going?" I asked swallowing hard and sitting back down onto the mattress.

He could barely look at me, it certainly wasn't the response I had been expecting or hoping for after last night. "Meeting some of the guys I went to school with," he said.

"It's not even eight in the morning." I looked at him, watching his body language, he was completely closed off. As he stood there, I suddenly felt very exposed and dirty. I reached for my clothes, the realization of what we had done last night hitting me again. I threw my shirt around me before dropping the blanket.

"Give me a minute and I will be out of here." I slid out from beneath the covers and walked into the bathroom, closing the door behind me. I turned the water on and ran my hands under the faucet, taking a handful and splashing my face with it. I was trying hard not to panic about Logan's demeanor. Maybe he was quiet because of the shock of what had happened between us or perhaps he was like this the morning after with everyone he had been with. How would I know? I swallowed hard as I studied myself in the mirror. I could see it in my eyes that something was different even with me. I looked different. I heard his phone ring, his muffled voice coming through the wall. I pulled my hair back in a ponytail, I needed to get my shit and get out of there.

As I stepped back out into the room Logan looked up from the chair, he held his phone in his hands. I went directly to my purse pulling out two pain relievers, ignoring the fact that he was staring at me. "You do know that what happened last night can't go beyond these walls, right?"

I swallowed hard at his words. I felt the tears building at his words, so I turned my back to him and wiped them away. "What do you mean?" I slipped my shoes on and grabbed my purse while waiting for his answer.

"I mean this, us, it was just a fling, because it can't be anything permanent, Leah."

"Just a fling?" I questioned, not quite believing what I was hearing.

"Well, yes, we're practically related. There can't be anything more between us than last night."

I didn't know what to say, and as I blinked, the tears ran

freely down my cheeks. After all that had happened between us last night, he had the nerve to say this now.

I pulled my keys out of my purse, grabbed my coat and walked to the door.

"I hope you understand."

I silently laughed to myself. "Oh, I understand, Logan. I understand that you really are just a bastard with no concept of how to treat someone appropriately."

I slammed the door behind me and left him standing in the middle of the room alone.

15
Logan

I spent the rest of Friday getting together with some of my old friends. It was great to catch up, and it was even better to drown my feelings in cold beers, food and laughter.

The day of the party, I sat in the driveway and looked at the house; I had come early to see if I could help with anything. I climbed out of the car, there was no more avoiding her, I would have to see her today whether I wanted to or not. I knocked on the front door and waited.

"Leah, Logan is here," Mom called from the hallway as I stepped inside.

"That's nice." I heard her voice call from the kitchen. She didn't sound too pleased to know I was there.

"Honey, why don't you go help her, I think she is a little overwhelmed. She refuses to let us help her."

I knew I was taking my life in my hands as I entered that kitchen. Before I said anything to her, I checked to make sure my mother wasn't following me. Leah stood with her back to me, working on a tray of food. I noticed she didn't have a knife in her hands, so I walked up and placed both my hands on either side of her small body, leaning onto the counter. "What do you need help with?" I whispered in her ear, practically grazing her neck with my lips I was so close to her.

"I don't need help, especially from you." She pushed my arm out of the way, moving to another part of the kitchen. She said nothing else, she didn't look at me, she continued preparing the food as if I weren't even there.

What did I expect? I knew I had hurt her but was else was I supposed to do. A girl like Leah, she deserved a relationship, but there couldn't be anything between us no matter how badly we wanted it.

I ran to the stove as a pot boiled over and went to turn the burner down when her hand reached out and collided with mine, forcing her hand into the way of the hot liquid. She pulled her hand toward her as the hot liquid splashed on her skin. She grabbed a towel, quickly wiping the hot water off.

"Let me see that," I said grabbing her arm.

"I told you to go," she said glaring at me. "I'm fine."

"Let me look at your hand," I said through clenched teeth.

"Why? You aren't a fucking doctor, Logan." Her eyes shot daggers at me as she stood there looking at me, the towel wrapped around her hand. The doorbell rang, breaking the silence.

"You want to be helpful, answer the damn door," she barked and turned to run her hand under cold water. I could already see a blister forming on her skin.

She had never been this harsh with me. Normally she was sucking up looking for approval not shoving me away. Although I had never fucked her and told her the next morning there couldn't be anything between us either. The doorbell rang again. "Never mind, Logan, I will get the damn door."

She threw the towel down and took a step but instead of letting her go I gripped her shoulders, turning her toward me. "I got the door," I whispered, looking into her eyes. She looked exhausted and hurt, a look I had never wanted to see in her, especially because of me.

After the confrontation in the kitchen, I kept out of her way by answering the door and mingling with the guests. Occasionally, Leah would wander into the living room carrying trays of sandwiches and desserts. She would smile and greet everyone, stopping to talk about one thing or another, but she never held an extensive conversation. Every time I got into her line of sight or was addressed in a conversation that she was having; her whole demeanor would change, and she found a reason to excuse herself to go back to the kitchen.

I offered to help her once again, figuring there was no way she would turn down the help or be mean to me in front of a houseful of people. But instead of making it public, she leaned into me and whispered a threat into my ear that involved the knife she held and my male member, that I took as a serious warning.

So, I kept my distance, and she kept hers. She made sure people had lots to eat and that their drinks were filled. Meanwhile, I spent the afternoon mingling with people I hadn't seen in years and watching her from across the room. The white dress she wore hugged all her curves I loved and had my hands all over only a few hours ago.

I watched as she brought out another plate of finger food and sat it on the table. She was just about to head back into the kitchen when Joe asked for people's attention. She stopped beside me and turned to face her father.

"First, I want to thank every one of you for being here to help celebrate ten years married to this beautiful woman. Anna has filled my life with happiness and love. I would also like to thank our children. Leah, you did a fantastic job of putting this all together and we want to wish you all the best in your new venture."

I frowned. Her new venture, where was she going? I raised my glass as Joe raised his to his daughter. She had said nothing to me, but then why would she. She owed me nothing.

". . . and to Logan, it's an absolute blessing to have you back here to celebrate this anniversary with us. We are both hoping you will come home a little more often to spend time with your mother and me. You have grown into a wonderful young man and we couldn't be prouder of you."

Yeah, you wouldn't think that if you knew what I did with your daughter a couple nights ago or how I broke her heart yesterday morning, I thought to myself as I nodded and raised the glass in my hand to them.

As the day went on more people came and went. By seven that night, there were only a couple people left. Joe and my mother were in the living room, the music played low while she rested her head against his shoulder as they danced together.

Leah came into the room, grabbed a few more plates and carried them into the kitchen. Her sad, tear-filled eyes finally met mine before she turned and walked away. Instead of just standing there, I grabbed a few dishes as well and carried them into the kitchen after her.

As I came around the corner, she stood against the counter gazing down into the sink looking like she was in pain. "Where do you want these?" I asked quietly.

"Just leave them on the counter, Logan. I told you, there's no need to help." She pushed herself away from the counter and got busy wrapping up the rest of the food. She put some of it in the fridge and then took the plates and loaded them one by one in the dishwasher.

"They seem really happy." I looked out into the living room where our parents were still dancing, there was no doubt about it, they were meant for one another. It had taken me this long to realize just how in love they were.

"Yes, they are. They are lucky to have found one another." She turned and looked at them, smiling. It was the first smile I had seen on her face since Thursday night.

"You organized a great party, Leah."

"Yeah, well, I figured they deserved it. I'm happy they are happy." She watched them longingly as they danced together. My mother's head still resting on Joe's shoulder. "It was the least I could do for them. They've both done so much for me, your mother has been so supportive of all my dreams," she said wiping a tear from her cheek as she smiled and continued watching them.

Joe held my mother close whispering something in her ear

and then kissing her gently. I couldn't help but glance over at Leah, the look on her face said everything she failed to say verbally—she was lost in her thoughts watching them, a soft smile on her lips. But the longer she watched the more her smile disappeared, and tears built in her eyes. She blinked hard and swallowed and I knew what she was thinking—she wanted what they had—but there was no way I was the man to give it to her.

"Leah, I'm sorry about what I said yesterday."

She cleared her throat, wiped her cheeks with the back of her hand and went back to cleaning up the plates on the table. "It's fine, Logan."

Who did she think she was fooling, her eyes lacked that glow she always had around me. I reached out and placed my hand on her shoulder. "It's not fine, please talk to me."

"I have nothing to say to you. You've made it crystal clear what this is, or I should say was. I can't do this right now." She shrugged out of my touch and walked across the kitchen to get away from me. I glanced over my shoulder at our parents who still danced in their own little world.

I walked over to where she stood, she wasn't about to get away from me that easy. I walked up behind her, placing both my hands on her waist. "Meet me tonight, at the hotel," I whispered in her ear. "Please. Let me fix this."

"Why so you can fuck me all over again and watch as I run away from you in tears? Do you even know how to fix this?"

"No, but I will try."

"I don't know."

"Please, Leah, don't make me beg. Just meet me."

She still didn't answer me and continued with what she was doing as if I hadn't said a word. "Leah, for fuck's sake, talk to me."

"I'll think about it, Logan. That's it." She wasn't playing, she was serious. I would have to wait and see if she showed up. She moved around the kitchen, cleaning, avoiding me completely even when I tried to help her. I didn't want to fight with her anymore, so I walked into the living room to say goodnight to my mother and Joe. They walked me to the front door.

"You are coming to brunch tomorrow, right?" my mother asked smiling.

I turned around and looked past them into the kitchen, Leah stood there leaning up against the door frame watching the three of us.

"Yes, I will be there," I said looking Leah directly in the eyes. I was hoping she could read what I was saying to her.

"Great, we will be there at eleven, don't be late." My mother leaned in and kissed my cheek. I hugged her goodnight and when I looked up, Leah had already left the doorway and a sinking feeling in the pit of my stomach told me she would not show up tonight. I walked out the door praying that my gut was wrong, and she would once again be laying in my arms.

I allowed myself to watch him as he walked out the front door. I had wanted him for so many years it was almost too much for me to take. When I heard those words come from his mouth after spending the night in his arms, I finally realized exactly where he stood. He wanted me too, just not in the same way I had wanted him.

This was all too much for me to process, it wasn't every day you had sex with the stepbrother you had fallen in love with. Obviously, I couldn't share this with my father or Anna, which made the whole situation worse. I even debated if I could share this with Jenna. But I had no choice, I didn't have a therapist which is technically what I really needed, and I had no one else I felt close enough to, so, Jenna was the lucky winner.

As I was putting more things away, I grabbed my phone and sent a message to her. She had moved and was now working in a different state. The time zones were different too, so timing may be tricky. I was hoping she would be finished work by now. Just as I hit send, both Dad and Anna walked into the kitchen. "Leah, honey, are you sure you don't want any help finishing up tonight?"

"No, Anna, I'm good. Please, go relax with Dad."

Anna gazed at me, a funny look coming over her face as she took two steps toward me. "Leah, are you sure you're all right, you're flushed, and you look upset. Joe, doesn't she?"

"Yes, she does, are you coming down with something?" Dad

asked while Anna placed her hand on my forehead to check for fever.

I smiled. "I'm just tired, so I will finish up here, then make a nice cup of spearmint tea and go relax with a good book. After all, you're always telling me how I need to do more of that."

My father let out a yawn and turned toward the living room. "I'm heading to bed," he said stretching and heading toward the stairway.

"Night, Dad."

Anna squinted her eyes at me, trying to figure out if I was okay or not. "If something is bothering you, you know you can talk to me," she said pushing away a couple strands of hair that had fallen into my face.

"I know." I swallowed hard. "Really I'm fine." At first, I wasn't sure she would believe me, I was sure it was written all over my face that something was wrong, but I was doing my best to pretend it wasn't. "Goodnight," she said finally.

"Goodnight," I said and watched as she followed my father up the stairs. I stopped what I was doing and rested both my hands on the counter in front of me and closed my eyes. Why did I go to his hotel? It had been hard enough before but having had that one taste of him to find out he didn't want me back ruined me.

I checked my phone and saw Jenna still hadn't responded. As always, when I needed her, she was nowhere to be found. I continued cleaning up, putting the last few dishes into the dishwasher. Then I washed down the counters, while thoughts of Logan ran through my mind. I could still feel the way he touched me, kissed me. It all still so fresh in my mind.

I wiped the counters again until there was nothing left to wipe and switched the kettle on, grabbing a mug from the cupboard. My phone vibrated on the counter while I was waiting for the kettle to boil. Jenna had finally gotten back to me, with two little words practically screaming at me on my screen. CALL ME.

I grinned at Jenna's response. It wasn't every day your best friend sent you a distress signal. I waited to call her until after I poured the boiling water into my mug and went down to the basement. I didn't want anyone to overhear our conversation. I sat in my dad's lazy boy, covered my legs with the blanket that rested there and flipped the TV on to help drown out the noise. Then, with my hands shaking, I dialed her number.

"Hey, buttercup, what's up?" Jenna's bubbly voice rang into my ear.

"Hey. I did it." My voice was void of all emotion it normally held. She would be able to tell something was wrong, I was sure.

"What did you do? What are you talking about?" she asked as I sat staring at the floor in front of me. I didn't know how to tell her and debated just hanging up before making a fool of myself more so than I already had. "Leah, are you all right?"

"Remember how I sent you a text and told you Logan came home."

"Yes, you told me you were going to poison him," she said laughing. "Oh my god, you didn't?" Her voice taking on a more serious tone.

"Worse." I could barely spit the words out of my mouth. "I slept with him." No sooner had the words fallen from my lips, the tears poured down my face.

I heard the screeching of brakes in the background, which pulled me out of my reverie. "Are you okay, Jenna?"

"I literally had to pull over, so I didn't crash my car. I think the signal cut out, who did you say you slept with?"

"Logan," I whispered.

"My god! What happened? How did it happen?"

"It just . . . happened. I went over to his hotel the other night and, like always, we argued and then the next thing I knew I was pushed up against the wall, his lips on mine. Then we moved to the bed, he was on top of me and well, one thing led to another."

"Just once, right?"

"Why does that matter?" I blurted into the phone.

"Maybe we can erase it from your mind. In case you forgot, I took that seminar on how to clear negative thoughts and events from your mind."

I rolled my eyes; this was so like Jenna and her gypsy ways. She had sat through a two-hour seminar on clearing your aura, karma, whatever you call it and she thought she could make everyone's pain go away.

"It was three times . . . still think you can work your guru magic?"

"Leah, what in the ever-loving fuck are you doing? Do you need to be reminded that he's your stepbrother? I mean I know you have crushed on him for years, but this is . . ."

"Don't tell me something I don't already know, Jenna, he already firmly reminded me of that."

"Of what?"

"What do you think? About three hours after he had finished completely blowing my fucking mind, he was very quick to remind me of who we were to one another and that it couldn't go any further than it already had," I said starting to panic all over again.

"Okay, Leah, calm down, so you slept with him, it's okay, it's over. I mean you didn't want to take it any further, right?"

I didn't answer her right away, all I could think about was the fact that I had wanted it to go further—much, much further. "What's wrong?" Her words in my ear pulled me back to the conversation at hand.

"His words were 'I'm okay with a fling, but nothing more, need I remind you that we are practically related.' Then tonight he invites me back to the hotel again." I couldn't help the tears that ran down my face. I was an absolute mess.

"Seriously, Leah, what a jerk. Please, don't go. Just put it behind you. You move in less than forty-eight hours. Even if you both wanted to, you wouldn't be able to get into a relationship with him now."

"Yes, I am leaving, but I'm moving to the same city he is living in, did you forget?"

"Does he know that?"

"No."

"Then keep it that way, protect yourself, girl. Don't go there tonight, let him stew in his own gravy for once. Stop letting him win. You've been giving into him since he and his mother came to live with you guys."

"What do you mean?"

"Look, for years he picked on you, even when he hurt you, you were always nice to him. After he moved, you wrote to him, practically begging him to write back, call or come home. I know that's why you always mailed him those letters. He's had you where he wanted you forever, right within arm's reach but never really touching you. The one time you don't send a letter, the one time you don't write, is the one time he comes back home. Coincidence, I think not. Let him chase you for a while, let him know what it's like to be on the receiving end of his own shit. Maybe then he won't be so quick to play these fucking games with you. Stepbrother or not."

I really listened to what she had to say. She was right, he had done exactly what she had said he did, and what she said about me was true as well. I couldn't see it until now. "Did you want me to call you tonight once I am home? We can have a Skype party; I'll just tell Jim we moved our girl's day."

"No, it's okay, it's been a long day. I'm going to drink my tea and go to bed."

"Promise me you won't go to him?"

"I promise," I said reluctantly. "If I even think about it, I give you permission to kick my ass before I leave."

"That's my girl." I hung up the phone, sat back in my dad's chair and closed my eyes.

I thought back to that first kiss we had shared those many years ago. That was the kiss that had sparked it all. I knew I liked him from the moment I laid eyes on him that day in the hallway at school, and after that kiss, those feelings had intensified.

With him being so far away, I guess crushing on him felt safer, but with Logan back home, I let weakness win. I couldn't do a fling; I had done plenty of those over the years. Once I was settled in my new career and a new home, I knew I would eventually find everything I was looking for. However, I secretly wished that Logan and I weren't related and that our parents weren't married, because I knew deep down that with him, we could have exactly what our own parents had taken years to find.

All the way back to the hotel, I prayed she would come to me. I'd had a taste of her, a taste of that sweet skin, those beautiful lips, her sexy body and I wanted more. Fuck, I wanted more, and I hadn't been able to stop thinking about the other night the whole time I was watching her today. Truth be told, I made a mistake by telling her that there couldn't be anything more between us and I felt like kicking myself in the ass. What happened between us had freaked me the fuck out. I hadn't expected to feel the way I did.

Back in my room, I turned the shower on and let the bathroom steam up. The only thing on my mind was her. I quickly showered and shaved and laid on the bed. I turned the TV on quickly finding something to watch. As I laid there mindlessly watching some crappy TV show, I thought back to her letters. I read them every chance I got, but I didn't have the guts to tell her that, or that I had kept them.

I heard a car door slam outside my window and jumped up to see if it was her. Sadly, it wasn't, and instead I watched a big burly man pull a suitcase from the trunk of his car. I needed to have her one more time before I had to return to Boston. Just once, and then I could void her from my system.

I grabbed my cell phone checking for messages, but nothing had come in. It was only nine o'clock, why wasn't she here? There was no way she was still cleaning up. I grabbed the room service menu and ordered a plate of chocolate-covered strawberries. She would love them, her two favorite foods combined into one. How did I know that? Because I fucking remembered. I remembered the cute little birthmark she had on the inside of her right thigh too.

"What the fuck is wrong with you?" I asked my reflection in the mirror. I feared she was not only in my head, but over the years she had worked her way into my heart. It was the little things, the way she touched me, the way she sucked on her bottom lip as I pumped into her and the way her eyes danced as she looked at me after it was over. She smelled and tasted so good she drove me near wild. "Where the fuck are you?" I said out loud, throwing my phone onto the bed.

I paced back and forth, finally stopping when room service knocked on the door. They placed the tray of strawberries on the little table and left. I stood looking at them then grabbed my phone and sent her a text message. I waited, staring at the screen. "Please, Leah, answer me."

However, that message went unanswered. Another hour passed, the strawberries I had delivered sat on the table, getting warm. They didn't appear to be as appetizing as I had first believed they would because I had hoped to be eating them off forbidden places on her body.

At two in the morning, I sent through one final text before I crashed into the mattress and fell into a deep sleep. I would see her tomorrow at brunch, there was no way she was getting away from me then.

18
Leah

I put the final touches on my makeup and then smoothed the wrinkles from my dress. I had deleted his messages as they had come in. He could beg me all he wanted. After my talk with Jenna, I knew it was time to take back my self respect. I hadn't slept last night, and it showed. I covered the dark bags under my eyes the best I could.

I placed the last few remaining items I still hadn't packed into my bag and zipped it shut. Dad had taken my luggage to the car while I grabbed my ticket and shoved it into my purse. In a matter of a couple hours, I would be on my way to Boston to start my new life.

"Leah, you're sure that is everything?" Dad asked as he walked into my room.

"Just this bag, Dad. That's it, my entire life packed up into a few bags." I smiled. It was a totally fake smile, I was sad I was leaving, but at the same time, I was so excited for what the future held. I needed to hold myself together for the brunch and once I was at the airport it would be over.

Dad wrapped me in his arms and pulled me against him. "You've made me so proud. I am so excited for you." I hugged him tight until I felt that familiar lump in my throat, I had been feeling it all night.

I pulled away as I heard Anna call from the bottom of the stairs, "We need to get going, I told Logan to meet us at the restaurant in half an hour."

Dad grabbed my bag from the bed and headed out the door.

"I'll be right down," I called after him. I just wanted to take a couple minutes alone.

The last name I had wanted to hear was Logan's. I sat down and just took in my room. All the memories it held. I contemplated writing a little note to Logan, to say goodbye, but decided against it. So I grabbed my purse and made my way down the stairs.

My phone rang on the way to the restaurant, Jenna's name flashed on the screen. I figured she would call today. Any good friend would call and check in. I was glad that I wanted to drive my car one last time before I sold it, so I was alone in the car. "Hello," I answered, my voice lacking enthusiasm.

"You all ready for your big move?" she asked trying to be excited.

"Yep, everything is packed and ready, my flight leaves at three."

"You're sure he isn't on the same flight, right?"

"Yep, Anna told me his flight leaves around eleven tonight. So, he won't even be at the airport at the same time. He'll probably bum dinner off my dad and Anna and then be on his way. By that time, I will be in my new apartment and on my way to a new life."

"All right, you sure you will be okay facing him this morning. I am booked in meetings all day, so I won't be readily available until after work."

"Yep, it will be fine. I've put my game face on. I'll be better once I am on that plane. I promise to call you once I am settled."

"Sounds good, you better come and visit soon, you won't be living far from me."

"I'll try. We'll Skype."

"Of course, take care, nut." I smiled. She had called me that ever since we met.

"You too. I love you."

"Don't go getting all sentimental on me. Talk to you soon,

safe flight and whatever you do, don't let him get inside your head . . . or your pants."

I laughed, but she had already hung up the phone. I turned the radio up and continued driving, almost passing by the parking lot of the restaurant. As I pulled in, I caught a glimpse of Logan entering the restaurant. He looked good, dressed in blue jeans and a black button-down shirt. I pulled into the first available parking space I saw and shut the engine off. I leaned back against the seat and took a deep breath. I wasn't in the mood for his games today, so he better not try anything.

I walked into the restaurant noticing my father and Anna already seated at the table with Logan. I smiled at the hostess and pointed to the table where everyone was sitting. "Sorry I'm late, Jenna called."

"That's okay, Leah, how is Jenna?" Anna asked, taking a sip of her tea.

"She is good." I reluctantly looked at the empty seat available between my father and Logan and debated asking my dad to move over so I could sit between him and Anna.

"Take a seat, Leah." I grabbed the back of the chair and went to pull it out, but Logan jumped to his feet and quickly pulled the chair out for me. Anna and Dad looked to one another surprised at his behaviour. I looked at Logan and scowled before I sat down.

"I already ordered for you. I got your favorite," Dad said as he rubbed my hand. "I also got you orange juice and a coffee."

"Thank you," I said tucking my purse at my feet. We listened as Anna resumed telling the story she had been in the middle of when I arrived.

The waiter finally brought out our food and placed the plates down in front of us. "Are you not speaking to me again?" Logan whispered in my ear.

"Good morning. Sleep well?" I smugly smiled back.

"Not really, but then I think you may know why."

"Leah, Logan, I want to say something," my father said grabbing Anna's hand.

We both looked to my father as if we had been caught with our hands in the candy jar. "Yes, go ahead, sir," Logan said grabbing his fork.

"We want to say how proud we are of you both. You were together under the same roof yesterday for the entire day and you didn't kill one another. It's a far cry from before."

"People change once they grow up and see the person for who they really are," I answered, grabbing my fork and digging into my blueberry waffles.

Logan looked at me and frowned. He glanced around the table to make sure no one was looking our way. "Really?" he mouthed. Everyone was busy digging into their food, so I smugly smiled at him, nodded, and shoved a forkful of food into my mouth.

I had made it all the way through breakfast with lots of eye-rolling and nasty comments. I couldn't help it, but every time he opened his mouth I wanted to hit him. I glanced at my watch, keeping track of the time as Dad took care of the bill and we waited for Anna to return from the ladies' room. I lifted my jacket from the back of my seat and went to put it on, but Logan grabbed it from my hands and opened the jacket for me to step into it. "Keep this up and they will wonder what is going on between us, Logan," I whispered to him.

He stood there looking at me, I could tell I was getting to him. I made the excuse of needing to use the ladies' room as everyone was leaving the restaurant so I could get away from him.

I'd asked Anna and Dad to meet me at the airport. I told them I wouldn't be far behind and watched as all three of them left. I ducked into the bathroom, quickly washed my hands and checked my makeup. Once I was sure they would all be gone, I made my way out the door. I was almost across the parking lot when I heard my name called from behind me. I didn't need to turn around, I already knew who belonged to that voice. "What do you want, Logan?" I huffed.

"Please, you've given me the cold shoulder long enough."

"I really don't think I have, to be honest." I stopped walking and turned around when I reached my car, sitting my purse on the hood. "What is it, Logan? I don't have a lot of time." I glanced at my watch; it was close to one.

"What do you mean you don't have time, I want to talk," he said stopping before me.

"Exactly what I said. I have a flight to catch, I can't be late."

"Yeah, about that, where are you going?" he asked looking down into my eyes.

I couldn't look at him, I knew I would end up buckling and telling him everything so instead I looked to the ground. "All you need to know is that I am leaving, you don't need to know where I am going."

"Please, Leah, just tell me."

"I have a new job, it's a new opportunity for me, a new beginning. This is a good thing for me. That's it, that's all you need to know." I stepped forward, took a deep breath and for whatever reason I placed a long lingering kiss goodbye on his lips. I felt his hands on my upper arms gripping me tightly as I pulled away. "I'll never forget what we shared, Logan. But for now, please do as I ask and leave me alone, let me get over you."

"What if I don't want you to get over me?" he questioned, speaking in a low sexy voice beside my ear.

"You should have thought about that before. I have to go."

I pulled out of his grip, grabbed my purse, climbed into my car and shut the door. I wasted no time as I put my key in the ignition, started the engine, and pulled out of my spot, driving away without looking back at him.

Three months, I had been back in Boston and not a single day had gone by that I hadn't thought of her. I could still see her face clear as day as she had looked up at me when she said goodbye, tears in her eyes. I dreamt of her every night and I could barely make it through a day without thinking of her or seeing something that reminded me of her. It was only getting worse as time passed, and once again at twenty-eight, Leah became the fantasy of my every masturbatory thought.

"Logan, Logan! Have you even heard a word I said? I'm waiting for an answer."

I blinked and looked at Jean as she stood in front of me. "I'm sorry, what?"

"You need to hire an interior designer for this house, Logan. It's stunning, but for me to feature it in the magazine, it needs to be decorated right."

My first thought was to hire Leah, if only she would answer the messages I had sent her. She would be perfect for this job.

"So, Logan? Who are you going to hire?" she asked marking down something on the notepad she had been carrying.

"Who do you work with that you would recommend?"

"A man in your position asking for a recommendation for interior designers? Surely you must know someone?"

"Look, I design the houses. Most of the time I don't even see it past the plans on paper." I shrugged looking around my new living room. I knew many designers, too many, most of them I had fallen into bed with after a drunken night of partying and ruined any sort of relationship. I wasn't going down that road again.

She let out a large sigh and wrote something else on her notepad. "All right, well, since you work for Jim and he is the one who wanted me to do the spread in the magazine on your home, I suggest that you contact Preston Interior Design here in Boston. They've recently hired a new designer. I have seen some of her work. She is fantastic, and exactly what I think you need here. She did work recently for the Boston Harbor Hotel and did an outstanding job." She pulled her phone from her pocket and shared with me some shots she had taken of the newly designed rooms. "I think if you call and tell Mary what you're looking for, she will put you in touch with her."

She pulled a card from her booklet and handed it to me. I looked down at it and shoved it into my pocket. "Call me once you are ready and I will get back here and do the spread. Jim is excited for you, he says you are the best architect in the firm right now and me doing this article on you will not only bring a lot of business to the firm, but I think it will catapult your career. People want different, and this is what they are looking for."

I smiled at her, took her card she had given me from my pocket and scribbled the name of the firm down on the back of it so I wouldn't forget. "I'll call first thing tomorrow."

"Let them know I referred you, it will save you the consult fee if not a little more. Call me as soon as you are ready."

I watched as she walked down the front walkway, her red hair swaying back and forth across her back, just as Leah's did. I shut the door to my new home and turned to look around. She was right about the house needing decor. I moved from a bachelor pad into a four-bedroom, open concept home. I could design them but decorating a house was a different story, I needed a professional.

I sat down in my living room and pulled my phone from my pocket. What were the chances that perhaps Leah would come to Boston and decorate my home for me? I let out a large laugh at the crazy idea. Then I thought, maybe it wasn't so crazy, and I should call my mom, she would know where Leah was. I quickly dialed the number.

It took three rings for her to pick up. "Hello."

"Hey, Mom, how are things?"

"Logan, I didn't recognize the number. I am good, how are you?"

"Good, Mom, listen. You don't have a number or an address where I can reach Leah, do you? Seems that she may have changed her cell number." The line went silent, and I heard her put her hand over the receiver and a few muffled voices in the background.

"Mom?"

"Sorry, honey, I don't. She asked that we keep that private."

"For goodness sake, Mom, I'm her stepbrother. I need to talk to her."

"I'm sorry, honey. I would do the same for you if you asked. Why don't you tell me what you need, I can pass on the message to her?" I let out a huff, even my mother was taking Leah's side.

"Don't worry about it. I have to go." We said our goodbyes, I hung up the phone and sat back in my chair thinking of how I would find Leah. I had no idea where she was, no address to write. I fucking missed her, she wouldn't leave my mind.

I was getting irritated with myself. I stood, walked into the kitchen and dialed the number to Preston Interior Design. I glanced at the clock noting they were probably already closed for the night. Seven rings, eight. "Hello. Preston Interior Design, Mary speaking."

"Yes, Mary, Jean from Dream Home Magazine recommended you. My name is Logan Lehmbeck, I'm one of the architects over at Jim's firm." I knew she would know who I was speaking of, we had often recommended Preston Interior Design to our clients.

"Ah yes, Logan. I've seen some of your work. I actually just finished doing work on a home you designed for the Meyers family."

I rolled my eyes. Meyers had been a huge pain in my ass during the whole design process. I didn't want to hear about what she did at the Meyers' home, I wanted to get this booked so I could get back to figuring out how I would find Leah.

"Anyway, I am calling because Jean thought you could set me up with a designer. She recommended the woman who recently worked on the Boston Harbor Hotel."

"Ah yes, she is a young spitfire. How about we set up the initial meeting tomorrow, if that works for you. I happen to have an opening at eleven. We can discuss what you're looking for, and if I think she would be a good fit then I will pass your account to her and she will call you to set up a meeting."

"Perfect," I said, gave her a bunch of information then hung up the phone and sat back down.

I flipped through the calendar in my phone and noticed that Mother's Day was in three days, then Memorial Day at the end of the month. *Two can play at this game,* I thought. I couldn't call or write, and since I didn't know for a fact that her cell number had changed, I would send her a text message every single day *except* holidays. And I would do it until she answered me.

I open a new text message, added her name to the top and thought for a moment before typing anything.

ME: IT'S RAINING, I HATE THE RAIN.

. . . and so began the way I hoped I would get her to talk to me again.

20
Leah

My day started with a morning from hell. I slept through my alarm—I never did that. I rushed around my apartment and got ready for work. I grabbed coffee and muffin on my way into work because I didn't have time for breakfast, and just as I was about to open the door to the office building some guy pushed on it from the other side, hitting my cup and spilling my latte right down the front of my brand new, white blouse. This day couldn't possibly get any worse.

It was now eleven, and I was finally seated in the safety of my office with the door closed, going through my email. I was just about to write out a reply when I heard my cell ping with a message. I frowned, only three people messaged me—Anna, Dad and Jenna—and if one of them messaged me at eleven in the morning, then something must be wrong. I bent and pulled my phone from the purse that sat under my desk by my feet and quickly punched in my password. I had three text messages.

I frowned, that's odd. They had come in over the weekend while my phone had been on silent while I worked from home. One on Saturday, one on Sunday and now one today.

LOGAN: IT'S RAINING, I HATE THE RAIN.

LOGAN: DID YOU KNOW THAT GINGERSNAPS ARE MY MOST FAVORITE COOKIE AND FOR A REASON I DON'T UNDERSTAND, THE GROCERY STORES HERE ONLY SELL THEM AT CHRISTMAS.

LOGAN: I ORDERED A CARAMEL MACCHIATO

FROM STARBUCKS THIS MORNING. I CAN SEE WHY THEY ARE YOUR FAVORITE!

I placed my phone down on my desk; I wasn't in the mood for his games. If he thought he would get my attention by sending me these stupid text messages, he was wrong. I let out a sigh and went back to checking my email when Mary walked by my office. She waved and then entered.

"Morning, Leah. How are you this morning?"

"I'm all right, sorry I was late, I had a latte incident on my way in."

"Oh dear, that doesn't sound very good." She laughed.

"No, it wasn't but I promise you I will make up the hours tonight."

"Don't worry about it, we work enough overtime here so there is no need to worry about such little things. Listen, Friday afternoon I had a preliminary meeting with a gentleman here in Boston. He works for one of the architectural firms here in Boston that we collaborate with. He has a brand-new house and after discussing what he thinks he wants done, I feel that you would be best suited for the job. He actually requested you, but I wanted to make sure that you would indeed be the best fit."

I frowned; I had only been working here for three months. I wasn't even out of my probationary period yet, I still had another fifteen days. They had assigned me one project, and it had taken me almost the whole time I'd been here to complete the work. It was impossible that anyone would know of me.

"He was referred to us by Dream Home Magazine and he specifically asked for the girl who did the re-design at the Boston Harbor Hotel. I told you that you did amazing work on that job. Anyway, his home is being featured in the magazine soon. This will be a big step for you."

"All right, great! Do you have his contact information?"

"Give me a few minutes to get back to my office, I will send you all of the information I gathered via email." I smiled, perhaps the day wouldn't be so bad after all.

Mary took off toward her office and I ran to the kitchen to grab another coffee before my next appointment came in. I was starting work on another large project. I had just sat down in my chair and was checking my email when Mary's message popped into my in-box. I had a funny feeling in my stomach as I opened the email and as soon as I saw the client's name I knew why.

I felt ill. Did he know it was me? I had specifically told everyone not to give him my number or tell him where I was. I was still staring at the name on the screen when my cell phone rang.

I grabbed the phone and answered the incoming call. "Hey, Leah, how are you doing, love." Anna's voice rang over the phone.

"Fine." It was the only answer I could muster as I sat staring back at the screen, Logan's name was the only thing I could see.

"You don't sound fine."

"Just having a bad day is all."

"I see. Do you have a minute? I wanted to talk to you about Christmas."

"Anna, it's only May." I frowned.

"It's your father, he wants to know if you are still planning on coming home."

"Anna, I don't know at this point. I'll have to see. Do you know if Logan is coming home?" Her answer to that question would dictate how I would respond. If he was going, I would spend Christmas alone in my condo with a tub of ice-cream and a bag of M&M's.

"I'm not sure yet, I didn't have a chance to ask him last week when I spoke to him."

Interesting, he called home last week, and now I was sitting staring at his name in little black letters on my screen. "Tell Dad that I will let you guys know closer to December." I got quiet for a moment then asked, "Anna, did you tell Logan where I am?"

"Heavens no. He asked about you though, asked where you were, but you requested that we keep it secret. I'm not sure why you wouldn't want Logan to know, quite honestly. I mean you live in the same city. I figured it may be nice for you to have someone to hang out with until you get to know people but if it's what you want . . ."

"It is . . . what I want," I said a little to quickly into the phone. I had no choice but to believe her, she had always done as I asked. While I continued to listen to her drone on, I quickly sent a reply to the secretary at the front desk and asked her to call Logan and book him in with another agent. I should have talked about it with Mary first, but I used the excuse that my calendar was too full to take on anymore clients. It wasn't and hopefully she didn't look and just did as I asked.

"Anna, your father would like you to promise to come home this year. He misses you."

"Can I let you know? I have a client waiting in the lobby for me. I have to go."

"Of course, dear. Chin up and try to have a good day."

I hung up my phone, shut my office door and pulled my privacy blinds down. I normally worked that way, less distraction, so it wouldn't give away anything. I sat back down at my desk, put my face in my hands and soon the tears poured down my cheeks.

I had done my best to forget about Logan, but lately he was all I could think about again. Now this. I wiped my cheeks and looked up at my screen. Mandy, the girl from the front desk, had responded. I clicked the email open and prayed as I read the words she had sent back.

"Unfortunately, Mary has already told me the appointment must stay with you. If there is a problem, you will need to speak directly with her. I already looked at your calendar and I penciled him in at the end of the month. Also, your one o'clock is here in the lobby."

I reread her email, suddenly feeling ill and I couldn't wait for this day to be over with. I composed myself as best I could, pulled open my consultation notepad and placed it on my desk. I smoothed my skirt, put on my best smile and walked out into the lobby to greet my next client.

21
Logan

Mom and Joe still wouldn't budge about Leah's location, but they had finally broken down and told me her cell phone number was still the same. So that meant she had been getting my texts, and I continued to text religiously every single day, minus the holidays. I was sure she would eventually answer, maybe even pick up on the pattern, eventually. She had no idea just how persistent I could be.

I could still feel the softness of her lips when I had kissed her, still smell the perfume on her skin as I pressed my face into her neck and I could still hear the sound she made while my face had been buried between her creamy thighs. I'd been a fucking fool. I hadn't had a date since I returned to Boston from the anniversary party, and I regretted everything I said to her that morning that made her run from me.

I thought back over the last few months. I felt like I was going a little crazy. I was sure I had seen her at numerous places around the city—like she was haunting me. Last month I followed a woman into a coffee shop one afternoon, sure it was her, only to find out it wasn't as I whispered dirty words into her ear. I got my face slapped for that one. I was at the grocery store one afternoon two weeks ago and thought I saw her again, so I followed her right to her car. When she stopped two security guards in the parking lot, I had to do some fast talking to get out of that one. I was almost certain I had seen her twice last week, but this time kept my distance.

I rolled over in bed and looked at the clock. It was just a

little after eleven and I still couldn't sleep. I grabbed my phone from the nightstand. Today had been the only day I hadn't messaged Leah since I started, but that was only because it was Yom Kippur. I planned to only text her on days that didn't have a holiday or observance.

I checked my calendar and noticed that I was supposed to meet with the interior designer from Preston tomorrow evening after work. My boss was breathing down my neck to get this shoot done for the magazine. Mary seemed positive about her choice of designers after our meeting a few weeks ago. I just prayed that she could get the job done right away and that I wouldn't have to wait several months.

If that was the case, Jim had already told me if this designer didn't work out, we would use one of our own. He wanted the spread in the magazine to happen sooner rather than later.

I scrolled through the pictures on my phone and came to the one I took the morning of the anniversary party. Leah stood beside me smiling, but it didn't quite reach her eyes. If I got another chance, I would give her exactly what she wanted, because I was miserable without her. I never thought those words would ever enter my head, the woman literally infuriated me all the time, but maybe that was what I loved about her.

I shut my phone off and threw it back on my nightstand. I closed my eyes thinking back to the night at the hotel. How I laid on the bed after we'd made love for the first time, she was curled up beside me. She didn't look at me, but I felt her fingers dance down to my already semi hard cock and take it into her hand. She ran her fingers over me, holding the weight of me in her hand and then letting me slip through her fingers, over and over until I was hard as a rock. Then she crawled under the covers and took me into her mouth, absolutely blowing my mind.

I felt the familiar throbbing now and took myself in my own hand, closing my eyes as I continued to think of her lips wrapped around me, her hand jerking me. I could still feel her run her tongue around the head of my cock repeatedly, her tongue piercing adding more sensation than I had ever felt before. I remembered exactly what I had thought of it when she showed me that piercing shortly after she had it done. It had been during her rebellious stage after we had all moved in together. When she stuck her tongue out to show it to me, I got hard just wondering what it would feel like to have her go down on me, but I was only in my teens and barely experienced.

A few more jerks and I felt myself let go, the hot, thick, white fluid shooting all over my abs. I cleaned myself off with the shirt that was lying on the side of the bed and rolled over, finally falling into a deep sleep.

I sat at my desk the next morning working on a house design for a retired couple, drinking my coffee, when my phone rang. "Hello."

"Mister Lehmbeck, this is Mandy from Preston Interior Design, I am calling to inform you that your appointment today will have to be rescheduled."

I couldn't believe my ears, there was no way I could reschedule this appointment. "I'm sorry?"

"Yes, sir, the designer who has been assigned to your project has had an unexpected design emergency come up."

"When will she be available?" I huffed into the phone.

"Not until the end of next month."

I glance at the calendar on my desk and scowled. That would be the end of June. "I'm sorry that will not work for me. I won't reschedule, so you tell her I will be at my property tonight, as previously agreed upon."

"Sir?"

"You heard me correctly. Tell her she is to meet me at my address when she's finished with her other appointment. I will wait." I hung up my phone, my head pounding. There was no fucking way I was waiting another day for the meeting, never mind a month. I was so pissed I couldn't even concentrate. I was tempted to call Mary to complain, but I doubted it would matter. I needed air, so I grabbed my jacket and ran down to my favorite restaurant for lunch.

I had found the place during my college years and brought all my friends here on a weekly basis for lunch. They had kept me alive during my school years—especially when I was sick—with their homemade soups.

The place was packed and as I scanned the room looking for a place to sit, a man stood up and left his table. I was pleasantly surprised a table was available when I saw a woman sitting behind him who very much resembled Leah. She wore a dark black sweater and she had her face angled down, but something in my gut told me for sure it was her.

She sat playing on her phone, slowly eating the bowl of soup in front of her and sipping on a tea or coffee. I rubbed my eyes to be sure I wasn't dreaming, but she was there.

"Hey, Logan, you eating in today? A table just opened, I need to clean it off, but if you want it, it's yours," Kathy said walking up to the counter.

"Give me a minute," I said, smiling to her.

"Sure thing, love. It's good to see you."

"You too, Kathy."

I took a deep breath and turned my attention to the girl in the dining area, watching her, she still hadn't looked up, but I didn't feel this way the other times I had thought I had seen her. It was Leah. I pulled my phone out of my front pocket and quickly sent her a text.

Leah

I had just finished playing a round of Candy Crush—my guilty pleasure I still used to relax when things were bothering me. Today, things were bothering me. Not only was I missing home, but I had spent my morning panicking about my appointment tonight. I took a sip of my tea and a mouthful of my soup when I saw a text message come in. I minimized my game and slowly read the words on my screen.

LOGAN: YOU REALLY SHOULD KEEP YOUR HAIR TIED IN A PONYTAIL, THAT WAY IT WON'T FALL IN YOUR SOUP.

I let out a laugh. Logan had been sending me these ridiculous random texts for almost a month. Some made me roll my eyes, others made me laugh out loud like I had just done, and others made me miss him more than I cared to explain. I shook my head and put my phone down and picked up my tea when a realization came over me. My hair was down, and I was eating soup. He was here, and he was watching me.

I swallowed hard, looked around the restaurant and saw him standing across the room. He wore dark blue jeans and a blue sweater that set his eyes off. He leaned up against the hostess desk, a sexy smile on his face, looking straight at me. I gave him a little wave, not sure if I should smile or not.

He said something to the lady standing there, pointed and walked toward me. My pulse quickened as I watched him weave his way through the dining room. I was beginning to feel faint when he finally stopped at my table. "What are you doing here, Leah?"

"Having lunch, what are you doing here?" I meant the remark to come out bitchy, but the shake in my voice totally gave me away and he smiled.

"Same. But what I meant was what are you doing in Boston?"

"I moved here four months ago. I didn't want you to know because I didn't want you to think I was coming after you. That's why I kept it quiet."

A waitress came to the table and took Logan's order. I studied him as he ordered; he looked better than he had when I last laid eyes on him. I kept getting gentle whiffs of his cologne and wished I could be back in his arms, resting my head against his chest, but I had already laid all the rules on the table. I had grown used to the fact that it wasn't ever going to happen again. I would not let it.

"Everything okay for you here, miss?" she asked me.

"Could I get another tea, please?" I asked. She nodded and stepped away from the table.

"So, are you working?"

How was I going to answer that? *Yes, I am working, I have an appointment with you in three hours that I tried to cancel, you bonehead.* Instead, I gently nodded. "I'm with a small interior design firm, nothing special." I wasn't about to let on who I worked for. He'd know soon enough.

"What part of the city are you living in?"

"I'm in a small apartment down by the water," I answered. "How are things with you? Did you get your house finished?"

"Things are good, really good. I got it finished, yes. I have an appointment with a designer tonight, they are featuring my house in Dream Home Magazine."

"Wow, that is amazing, Logan. You should be so proud."

He shied away for a moment and then quietly spoke, "Truth is, I wanted you to design it. I tried to find out where you were. I even called my mom to see if she would give me your number, but she refused."

"Well, we can't always have what we want, now can we," I bit back. They were his words not mine, and I would make him swallow them.

Things went well once we were done with our usual bickering. Logan insisted on paying for my lunch, so I let him. We walked together to the lot where I had parked my car. I pressed the button for the remote start as we continued across the lot. I turned to him when I got to my car. "This is me," I said. "Thank you for lunch."

"You are welcome. It was my pleasure."

Our eyes caught and I could see something unreadable in his. I wanted so badly to kiss him, but I needed to be strong, I wasn't getting involved with him again. He studied my face, a faint smile coming to his lips.

"Before I go, are you doing anything this weekend? Perhaps you would like to see a movie?"

I thought for a moment and swallowed hard. If he thought anything had changed, he was wrong. I had laid everything out on the line and told him what I wanted and either he agreed, or he didn't. Just because we now lived in the same city, I wasn't about to be his toy when he was lonely.

I didn't want to lead him on but, at the same time, a movie would be great. I had barely gotten anytime to know this city. I however didn't trust myself in a dark theatre with him. "How about coffee and dessert tomorrow night instead?"

A sexy smile came over his face, but I stopped him before he could say anything. "Nothing has changed, Logan. I meant what I said before, it's all or nothing." I leaned into him and gave him a hug and a small kiss on the cheek, "See you tomorrow. Text me the address." I got into my car and headed back to the office.

22
Leah

I sat in my office doodling on a piece of paper and staring at the clock. I had to be all business in less than forty-five minutes, and since lunch, I had been anything but all business. I was a blubbering idiot by the time I got back to the office. I called Jenna and cried to her for over an hour after I had returned, instead of working on a few projects that were due for Monday.

After seeing him at lunch, I had been thrown into a whirlwind of memories. The want for him so high I had become a basket case. Jenna tried her best to talk me down and come up with a way to get out of this appointment with him, but I couldn't do it. How unprofessional would it look to my boss? I had no choice but to suck it up and stay professional because there was no room for weakness. *If I was going to go I had to leave now,* I thought to myself. I packed up my bag, wrapped my coat around me and headed to the front door.

"Leah, I forgot to tell you, I couldn't cancel your five thirty," Mandi said as I walked by her desk.

"It's fine I'm on my way now. If Mister Lehmbeck calls tell him I am on my way."

My nerves were getting the best of me the closer I got to his address and as I drove up the long circular driveway, I was sure I would have to stop so I could be sick. But as soon as the house came into view, the sick feeling fell away and my jaw dropped open. It was the most stunning design I had ever laid eyes on, and it should be in a magazine.

I slowed my car and just looked at the house taking it all in.

I saw his truck parked out front and I pulled my car in behind his, hoping he hadn't seen my vehicle pull up. I slowly got out of the car, taking my laptop and phone with me and I walked up to the front door and rang the bell.

I turned to look at the front yard. This place was a little oasis hidden up a long driveway buried in the trees. Logan had done well for himself. I turned around just in time to have the front door pulled open and saw Logan standing inside the door. The look on his face was one of shock.

"What are you doing here?"

"I came for my appointment with Mister Lehmbeck," I answered, swallowing hard, trying to keep the look of want from my face.

He stood there not knowing what to do. "Mister Lehmbeck, it would be easier if you let me in to see what your place will need."

"Cut the crap, Leah, what are you really doing here?"

"Mister Lehmbeck, you may call me Miss Tate. Do I have to remind you, you are the one who requested this appointment with Preston Interior Design?"

He looked at me as if I were kidding but when my face showed no signs of a smile, he stepped to the side and let me in.

I stepped into the foyer, removed my shoes and looked around. The house was a blank canvas and I was secretly excited to get started.

"Seriously, Leah, what are you doing here?"

"You called Preston Interior Design and requested the designer who completed the work at the Boston Harbor Hotel, didn't you?"

"Yes, but—"

"Well, you got her. Now, if you wouldn't mind showing me around."

Logan's jaw dropped as I spoke. "Why didn't you tell me that today? You said you were working for some small firm."

I pulled my phone from my pocket getting the camera ready

to take pictures. "Because I didn't find it important, now where would you like to start?"

"You didn't find it important to tell me you were working for one of the largest design firms in Boston, or make any comment when I told you I wanted you to do the design for me?"

I ignored him and walked further into his home. I was already making notes, color ideas, style and lighting.

"Leah, are you going to answer me?"

"It's Miss Tate. Now please, Preston charges two hundred dollars an hour for consultations. I don't want to waste your time or money, Mister Lehmbeck. Are we going to get started?"

Once Logan started showing me around, I noticed how well the house flowed and the more excited I got.

It was a little after seven by the time we entered the kitchen, the last room of the tour. I dropped my notepad onto the island and continued making more notes. I was just about finished when Logan stepped up beside me.

"So, do you think you can fix me up here?" he asked.

"Yes, I do. Give me a week or two to get my ideas together and then my team and I will get started," I said, keeping my eyes trained to the paper.

I heard him exhale and then he leaned against the island and cleared his throat. "Leah, why haven't you looked at me once since you got here?"

I took a deep breath, closed my eyes and continued writing. "Mister Lehmbeck, I told you, it's Miss Tate to you. I am here to do a job, not flirt like you have been doing with me for the past two hours. Now, if you want me to do this job for you . . ."

"Fine, Miss Tate, I expect to see your completed designs this coming Friday, no later. I assume you know the way out."

I didn't have a chance to say anything before Logan left the room. I could feel anxiety building within me and knew it would only be a few more moments before I would be in tears in his kitchen. The whole night he had subtly been placing his hand on my lower back as he guided me into the rooms, and he would find some little way to touch me. And every single time he touched me, I felt that familiar ache between my legs, making me wet, and sending my heart into a racing mess to the point where I could barely breathe.

I slid my notepad back into my bag and slipped my shoes on, making a mental note to make sure I had my assistant present for other meetings. I reached to open the closet, pulled my coat off the hanger and as I shut the door, Logan's reflection appeared in the mirror. Our eyes met, and I knew instantly that whether he liked it or not, he felt the same way about me as I did him. We said nothing, we just stood and stared for a couple of minutes, eyes locked on one another.

I bent to pick up my bag, and that was when he stepped up behind me, reaching down and grasping the handle at the same time I did, our hands colliding. I let the bag go, and he held the door for me and walked me out to my car. He placed the bag in the trunk and slammed it shut as I walked around to the driver's side. He opened the door for me and when I went to climb in, but his hand gripped my upper arm. "Seven, Friday night. I'll see you here."

"Yep." That was all I was going to get out of my mouth.

He went to say something, but I cut him off. "Goodnight, oh and about the dessert plan for tomorrow, let's pass." I got into my car, pulled the door closed, started the engine and threw the car into reverse. I drove down the long circular driveway, everything blurring in front of me as my hands shook. I stopped just before I had to turn onto the road and placed my head on the steering wheel. I didn't know what the hell I was even doing here, I couldn't work with him.

My phone rang, causing me to jump. I reached in my bag and pulled it out seeing Jenna's name on the screen. I wiped the tears from my cheek and answered the call. "Hello, darling," I sang in a fake voice.

"Oh, no."

"What?"

"I was too late. I meant to call before you had your meeting or during, but I lost track of time. I was planning to be your decorating emergency." She let out a laugh while I held back my tears. "How did it go?"

"All right," I lied, "I will meet him again this Friday at seven to go over my plans."

"I see, at your office?"

"No, at his place."

23
Leah

After my breakdown with Jenna, I went home and soaked in a hot bath with lavender essential oils and Epsom salts. I also downed two bottles of merlot and called in sick the next day.

I spent the rest of the week working tirelessly on his design. Not only because it was for him, but it was also because they would feature this project in a magazine that could essentially make or break my career.

It was Friday, and I had just returned to my desk with a fresh cup of coffee and a warm chocolate chip cookie and sat back down to complete my reports for Logan. I pulled the blinds to stop the sunlight from beating on my computer screen, my head pounding. An email notification popped up on my screen. I opened the email and read.

Miss Tate,
We need to reschedule our meeting tonight to eight pm.
Mr. Lehmbeck

I let out a laugh. Maybe I had been a little too serious over the whole "we need to be formal" nonsense as I read his email. I hit reply.

Logan,
My day started at four am, the earlier the better.
Leah

I went back to the screen I was working on and suddenly another notification popped up. I quickly switched screens and read.

Miss Tate,

How dare you address me as anything other than Mr. Lehmbeck. This job is important to us both. I will see you at eight.
Mr. Lehmbeck.

I texted my assistant to let her know to meet me at Logan's address, but she responded back almost immediately telling me that she had a prior engagement and couldn't make it. I let out the breath I had been holding as my stomach sank. I would have to do this meeting alone.

I shut my email down, there was no way I would win an argument of any size with him, he was too stubborn, besides this was my idea. I continued to work away and by six I was just finishing up. I had enough time to go home and quickly change before I had to drive out to his place. I printed the designs and packed them up for tonight.

I stopped just around the corner from Logan's and picked up two coffees. It was exactly what I would have done for any other client I was working with, he shouldn't be any different. I slowly drove up the winding driveway and pulled my car up beside his truck.

I took a breath before climbing out of the car and pulled out the bag containing the presentation. I rang the bell, standing there holding the coffees in one hand, bag flung over my shoulder. As soon as the door opened, Logan stood in front of me in blue jeans and a white button-down shirt, open at the collar. He looked so crisp and clean and as I walked in and past him I caught a whiff of his cologne, the same cologne he had worn that night. I could smell something cooking and tried hard to ignore it, but my stomach gave me away by letting out a loud groan. I was starving.

"Hungry?" he asked leaning up against the wall.

"Let's get started, shall we." I smugly smiled and handed Logan our coffees. I removed my shoes still carrying my bag.

"We should go into the kitchen, it's lighter in there with the proper space to lay everything out."

"No, I don't think so," he said walking into the living room.

I looked after him, always the stubborn one, but I followed him into the living room without complaint. I put my bag down, pulled out my presentation and opened the section where I kept his designs. I lay them on the small table, and began with the room we were in.

As I went over the designs with Logan, I noticed he wasn't saying too much, he either liked them or hated them, I couldn't tell. He let me get through about five rooms before he made any kind of comment.

"I don't think these will work, Miss Tate. I like nothing about modern designs."

"Mister Lehmbeck, may I remind you, you've designed a modern home, and you were very quick to tell me that modern design was not only what you liked, but what you wanted."

"I don't want to live in a home I am afraid to touch. This is a perfect image for something that will be printed in a magazine, not lived in."

I ignored the comment and continued onto the next few rooms, each one he quickly dismissed. I was getting rather flustered which didn't happen often, but I had never gone back to a client and have them turn away almost all my suggestions.

"Let's see what is next," Logan demanded impatiently.

As I flipped to one of the last three rooms, explaining what we would do in the third bedroom, he picked up the design and threw it to the side. He then picked up the last two rooms and threw them down. "These will not do, Miss Tate."

"Mister Lehmbeck, you gave me exactly one week to design the whole interior of this house. It was you that put me on a rushed schedule. Now if this isn't up to your standards then perhaps you will need to find another designer or tell me what it is you truly want."

I couldn't help it, he was doing this on purpose, I knew it, he knew it and I knew he knew that I knew it. There was nothing wrong with what I had done, I had decorated this house to what he told me he had wanted during our consultation.

He was just about to come up with a rebuttal when the smoke detector beeped loudly. His eyes went wide, and he ran into the kitchen. I frowned wondering what the hell was going on and followed him quickly into the kitchen.

My eyes almost fell out of my head when I rounded the corner. The reason we couldn't go into the kitchen was right before my eyes. Dirty dishes were every where, covering every surface, and Logan stood by the oven waving a towel in front of the door to dissipate the smoke that was pouring out. I tried my best to keep a straight face at the whole scene.

He turned to look at me and that was when the second over door began spewing smoke. "Fuck fuck fuck." He shut that portion of the oven off and cracked the door, smoke billowing out. I ran for a window and cranked it open to help clear the air.

I glanced to the tiny round table in the breakfast nook and saw two place settings, candles and a bottle of wine chilling in the center.

"I didn't know you were having company. Perhaps that is why you liked nothing I had done because you were rushing to get rid of me. We could have just rescheduled tonight."

"I'm not. I was making you dinner. That way we could continue to go over things together afterwards. You said your day started at four and you canceled our dessert date last night, so I figured I'd feed you."

I looked around and gave a small smile. Logan standing in front of the mountain of dishes and a complete mess of a stunning kitchen. "I see. Did your mother not teach you anything?"

"I never took much interest in learning how to cook, Gingersnap." He shrugged and looked around the kitchen at the mess that was before us.

"Let's face it, Logan, I mean Mister Lehmbeck, you hate everything I have done." I could feel my face getting hot. I was exhausted, frustrated, and the idea of having dinner alone with him, with wine was far more appealing than it should have been.

I drank back the last of the wine and relaxed back on the couch as Logan looked over all my designs again. "You don't really hate them all, do you?" I questioned.

"Honestly, I think they are great."

"You do?" I normally let none of my insecurities show but here they were out in full force. The glass of wine I drank wasn't helping.

"I do. I can't wait to get started. How long do you think it will take before everything is finished?" he asked finishing his glass of wine.

"When do you need it by?" I asked, reaching for my phone.

"The end of the month," he said looking down at another rendering.

"No worries. I'll get ordering things right away. Call your photographer back and book in your shoot." I glanced at my watch. "I should get going, it's late," I said shoving my phone back into my bag.

Logan stood and helped me up off the couch. As I went to turn, I almost fell, Logan reached out and grabbed me around the waist, steadying me. He pulled me back against his chest and let me rest there, holding me. I closed my eyes, the feel of his chest behind me was so comforting. His large strong hands still sat on my waist even though I was now fine. I felt his lips at my ear and a warm puff of breath on my neck.

"I think maybe I'll take you home," he whispered.

The light-headed feeling returned as I felt my pulse quicken. "I don't think that is a good idea," I whispered back. I should have moved, but I didn't. Instead, I stood there taking in the feeling of my body pressed to his.

He leaned his head into my neck. "You smell so good," he whispered, his one hand left my waist to pull my hair back away from my face. The feel of his rough fingers against the skin of my neck, sent a shock of energy through my body, hardening my nipples. I felt his breath on my neck, the hot puff of air as he breathed, and then I felt his lips on my earlobe. His teeth grazed the bottom. "I want you so bad."

I closed my eyes and let my head fall to the side, letting him have full access to my neck. As he kissed his way down, he gently pulled the collar of my shirt off my shoulder, exposing my bare skin to him. His lips gliding over my skin. His hand left my waist and found its way to my breast, gently squeezing it. I felt a rush of heat to my center. I turned and met his lips, as he squeezed my breast he deepened his kiss, his tongue forcing my lips apart. He wasted no time, his fingers gingerly unbuttoned my shirt, he slipped the cups of my bra off my breasts and ran his thumbs of my already hardened nipples as he devoured my mouth.

He pulled away from my mouth and looked at me and when I didn't protest, he bent down and ran his tongue and teeth over each hardened nipple, sending shock waves through my body. While his hands continued to caress and fondle my breasts, he met my mouth again, this time totally losing me in his kiss. His large hands ran through my hair cupping the back of my head, his tongue swept through my mouth.

The sudden ring of my phone brought me back to reality. I jumped out of Logan's arms, quickly covering myself up and turned in circles looking for my phone. I reached for it, fumbling it in my hands. "Hell, Hello."

I swallowed, embarrassed that someone had caught us. I pushed my hair out of my face trying to regain my composure. I was so warm, and my eyes connected with Logan's as I heard Jenna's voice come through on the phone.

"I'm just about home," I lied, fastening the buttons on my shirt. "Can I call you back once I am inside?" As soon as I heard the answer, I ended the call, grabbed my bag and made my way to the door. I left Logan standing there, the outline of his raging hard on through his jeans staring back at me.

"I will drive you, hold on." I heard his voice from the other room. I closed my eyes and threw my coat and shoes on, in a rush to get away.

"It's good I'm fine, really," I called.

"Leah, you are not fine. You've had a lot to drink, I will drive you."

"I'm fine, I only drank one glass of wine. I will call you in two days with a delivery schedule. I'll talk to you soon."

I pulled the door open in a rush and ran from the front door to my car. It only took a matter of seconds to drive toward the long winding driveway. Just before my car started its descent down, I looked in my rear-view mirror to see Logan standing in the doorway watching me drive away.

24
Leah

I drove all night to get to Jenna's, debating the whole time whether I should come and see her or not. I could handle all this on my own, but I needed my best friend. I pulled in her driveway and shut the car off, it was only four in the morning and her house was still bathed in darkness. Did I go and knock or just sleep in my car? I thought on that for a minute and then I saw a light come on in the kitchen window and saw a messy haired Jenna in the window. Thank god.

I flicked the lights on my car to get her attention and she soon looked out the window. I got out of the car and held up my cell phone with the screen on waving it frantically, something we used to do as kids when we were trying to alert one another without our parents finding out. Suddenly the door opened, and she stepped out on the front porch. "Leah? What are you doing here?" she whispered waving for me to come to her. As soon as I got to her, I fell into her arms, tears falling from my eyes.

"I had to come, I needed to spend time with you. I don't know what else to do."

"About Logan?"

"Yes."

I cried into her shoulder, I was utterly exhausted and all this with him wasn't helping.

"Well, come on in, it's freezing out here." She let me go and pulled open the door ushering me inside. "You must be exhausted."

"It was just a short six-hour drive, I left as soon as I got home."

"Well, short drive or not, you need to sleep. I will get you a blanket and set you up in the guest room. Jim will be leaving soon, and I will call in to work with a family emergency." Jenna, unlike me, worked on weekends.

I followed her to the spare room, careful not to make any noise and fell onto the couch pulling the pillow under my head. I was exhausted, my body ached. Jenna walked quietly into the room and draped a blanket over me and leaned down kissing me on the forehead then shut the door. I fell into a deep sleep.

By nine I was awake and sitting on the living room floor, cross legged, watching *Ellen* and delving into a container of Ben and Jerry's Coffee Toffee Bar Ice Cream for breakfast. I shoved the sweet, ice-cold dessert in my mouth and closed my eyes savoring the flavor. It felt good to just relax. Jenna came in and sat across from me. "Okay, we are alone now. Spill it."

"Seriously, Jenna, Mary is going to kill me if she finds out about that kiss." I was crazy with nerves and I never should have made the drive to Jenna's, but I needed my best friend. I shoved another mouthful of ice-cream in my mouth.

"Well, you can't take it back now," she said shoving a handful of M&M's in her mouth.

"You're not going to see him alone next time, right? You are taking someone with you?"

"I emailed my assistant, she is to go with me next time. I am sure Logan is going to be pissed."

"Serves him right, Leah, don't worry about it." It didn't matter the amount of permission she bestowed upon me, I still felt like shit and I knew better. I was supposed to be professional.

Suddenly my phone started to ring, and I glanced at the screen.

"Who is that?" Jenna asked reaching for my cell phone, but I pulled it away from her reach.

"It's Logan. He has been calling me for the past few hours. What should I do?"

"Best to let it go to voice mail, don't you think?"

I looked at the screen, my heart telling me to answer, but I knew Jenna was right. I sat the phone down beside me and averted my eyes from her, trying to hide how I truly felt.

"I'm not going to let you drown your sorrows this way. Come on, let's put all this sugar away and head to the spa. We can soak in the plunge pools and get a massage by a hot young man." She ripped the container of ice cream from my hands and picked up the tray covered in nothing but refined sugar. I stood following her with our coffee cups.

"I don't have a bathing suit."

"Duh, you can borrow one of mine. Let's go."

An hour later, we were already soaking in one of the hot tubs while waiting for our massages. The spa was empty, and we had all the pools to ourselves. "So, tell me, is he any good?" she questioned.

"Who?" Even though I already knew who she meant, I thought I had better clarify.

"Logan, who do you think?"

I blushed at her question. "Probably the best I ever had."

"Hmmm who would have thought. Do you love him? Like really love him."

I hesitated. I did love him, I just wasn't sure I wanted to share that information.

"You don't need to say anything. I can tell. Do you remember all those years ago when you broke up with Aaron?"

I smiled thinking back to how funny the whole situation was now. "Of course."

"You did know he really only wanted to date Kara Kingsley, right. That he made up the story of there being a rumor to get out of the relationship with you."

"How do you know that?"

"You didn't show up the next day for school, so I asked

Logan where you were, he said you were home sick with food poisoning. When I was on my way out of fourth period, I saw a whole bunch of people surrounding what appeared to be a fight. I ran over to see what was going on, you know how I loved a good scrap. I was shocked to find Logan and Aaron going at it. Logan had him pinned to the ground. He kept shouting at him to tell him the truth, he wouldn't let him get up until Aaron confessed. He just kept punching and kicking him."

My eyes widened. "He got himself suspended from school for that fight, I remember that."

"Yep, Mister Turner, the science teacher, broke up the fight. Logan had broken Aaron's nose and arm."

"Yep, Aaron was pissed."

"They marched Logan and Aaron to the principal and called your parents. They suspended Logan on the spot for two weeks."

"He never told anyone what that fight was over either. He just said it was nothing they needed to concern themselves with. I guess he wouldn't even tell the principal. He got into so much trouble when that happened, and it was all because of me?"

"Yep, he told me that Aaron finally confessed to him in the principal's office that he lied to you. There never was a rumor."

"Why are you only telling me this now?" I asked.

"Because, even though I see what he is doing to you by playing these games, I think you also need to know that he really does care for you on some sort of level that maybe you are fighting not to see."

"Ladies, your masseurs are ready for you now." I looked up to see a spa attendant standing there.

"Great. Thanks."

We pulled ourselves from the water and entered arm in arm into the change room. "Just so you know, I am supposed to comfort my friend when she is upset. Even though I hate to see what he has been doing to you, I see you love him, and I think its only fair that you have the entire picture in your head when you make the decisions you are about to make. Now go and enjoy having man hands all over your body for the next hour. I'll see you soon." She flicked a towel at me, smiled and left the change room in her robe and slippers.

The smell of lavender soothed me as I lay in the darkness, while Nick, my masseur, found every teeny tiny knot in my aching muscles. I closed my eyes and listened to the soft music that floated in the air, my mind drifting to Logan.

As soon as my massage was over, I went to my locker and checked my phone. My assistant had called and left me a message regarding Logan's order. Then I listened to Logan's messages. I was just stepping into the shower when Jenna came through the door looking relaxed as ever.

"I am jumping in the shower and then I have to go," I stated to my sleepy faced best friend.

"Go where? We are supposed to have lunch here too."

"No time, I need to get back. I have work to do and my assistant needs my help. I should at least be in town to do that."

Jenna smiled and wrapped her arms around me. "I miss you so much," she said into my shoulder.

"Me too, babe, me too."

25
Logan

It had been four days since Leah had left my house running like a mad woman. I hadn't heard a word from her. I was hoping she would have texted me when she had gotten home but there was nothing from her. I leaned back and looked down at the design I was working on, everything about it was wrong. I was frustrated, in more ways than one, and this project wasn't helping matters.

My phone rang on my desk, I reached for it hoping it was Leah. "Hi, Logan, it's Jean."

I searched my mind: Jean, Jean. Why couldn't I think of who Jean was?

"From Home Design Magazine."

"Oh, yes, sorry you caught me in the middle of something," I said brushing off the fact that I couldn't remember who she was.

"I received your message. Let's book you in for that shoot on the first of the month. That way it will give us plenty of time to get you as the featured guest in the following month's issue."

I glanced at the calendar that sat on my desk. I had no clue what the date even was and since I hadn't heard from Leah, I couldn't exactly fight her on this. After all, I was the one who had called her looking for the date. "Sounds good."

"Great, see you then. I should be there about three. Oh, and please make sure the designer is there too. I would like to include her in on the shoot."

Leah would kill me for agreeing to have her there. "No problem," I said lying through my teeth, I'd worry about it later. I hung up the phone and tried to concentrate on the design I was working on. Instead, I sat and stared at it, so I pushed that project to the side and started to work on another one, but the same thing happened. Lines blurred and nothing was clear.

I grabbed my coat and was about to head down to the coffee shop when the phone rang on my desk. I contemplated not answering it but reached for it anyway.

"Logan."

The other end was silent for a moment and then I heard a small weak voice. "Hi, Logan. It's Leah."

"Hi." I sat forward, my pulse racing at the sound of her voice.

"The painters will finish up soon and I have the first furniture shipment coming in on Friday. I'm expecting the rest to be there next week then our work will be finished."

A funny feeling came over me at her words. I didn't want to be finished with her. "What time do you need me to be home for the delivery?"

"I don't need you there per se. I'll get the keys from the painters, and once all the furniture is moved in, I will lock the house up before I go. Once everything is complete, I will leave the key in the mailbox outside the front door."

I didn't know how to respond to what she said, it sounded like she didn't want to see me.

"Does that work for you?"

I wanted to say many things, tell her the truth about how I felt. "Okay. No problem." The words fell quickly from my lips. In all honesty, it was a big problem.

"See you Friday morning." As quick as her call had come in, it was over, and I sat listening to a dial tone. She was gone.

I hung up the phone, grabbed my keys, shut the lights off in my office and made my way to the coffee shop.

Later, as I drove up my driveway, all that was on my mind was Leah. I kept thinking back to the night when all I had wanted to do was continue to kiss her into the morning, nothing more, but that damn phone of hers had to ring, pulling her from me and back into reality.

I slammed the front door shut and walked into the living room. I threw the fireplace on and flopped onto my old couch, turning the TV on as I sat down. I closed my eyes as the TV echoed in the large empty space. Soon, this space would be transformed, and it would all be because of her. I would have her design as a constant reminder of what I wanted the most: her. I would live here surrounded by her, wrapped in her, without her.

I needed to tell her she was the one, without just coming out and saying it. She wouldn't believe me if I did. She would be here tomorrow morning at eight. Noting the time, I had less than twelve hours and needed to get busy with my plan.

26
Logan

The sun shone through the window of the breakfast nook as I sat eating my oatmeal and reading through the morning paper. I heard a car door slam and felt my stomach hitch at the thought of seeing her this morning. I had been up almost all night deciding how to go about this and I was excited to see the look on her face. I got up from the table and carried my bowl to the dishwasher, quickly loading both my mug and bowl into the top rack. Finally, the doorbell rang, and I made my way to the front door. I smiled as I pulled the door open only to come face to face with a girl I had never seen before.

"Mister Lehmbeck?"

"Yes."

"I'm Susan." She stood there holding her hand out smiling at me as if I should know who she was. When she realized I had no clue, the smile disappeared, and the hand dropped. "I'm Miss Tate's assistant. She is sorry she had to deal with something before arriving this morning, but you need not worry. She has sent me in her place, and I have everything under control. She should be arriving in the next forty minutes or so."

"Where is Miss Tate? I've asked that she personally handle this account." I sounded like an utter dick and I knew it, but I was pissed.

"I'm sorry, she was dealing with an issue regarding one of your pieces. I had a voice mail on my phone this morning asking me to be here at eight." The girl gave me a gentle smile. "The first delivery will be here in about ten minutes, Mister Lehmbeck."

"Yes. Come in." I stepped to the side and let her in. "Miss Tate told you I have meetings to attend this morning, so I won't be here to oversee things."

"Yes, sir." She sat her briefcase on the living room table and pulled her laptop out of her bag. "She gave me instructions to follow until she could get here."

I was a little uncomfortable leaving her here alone, and I wondered where the hell Leah was. This was what cell phones were for. I would have canceled the few meetings I had if I didn't have to be there in thirty minutes.

"There is coffee in the kitchen. Help yourself. I will be back as soon as I finish my meetings." She smiled up at me as she dialed a number on her phone and spoke to someone about the deliveries today.

I grabbed my jacket from the closet. As soon as I was in my car, I dialed Leah's cell. If she thought I would put up with this shit, she was wrong. I waited for it to connect but after only two rings her phone went straight to voice mail. "You've reached the personal voice mail of Leah, leave me a message."

"Leah, where the hell are you? Call me back." As I hung the phone up, I felt the tension in my jaw getting worse as I drove down my driveway. I quickly dialed her office.

"Hello Preston Interior Design."

"Hi, Could I speak with Leah Tate, please." I flicked my thumb on the steering wheel as I sat at a red light.

"May I ask who is calling?"

"Logan Lehmbeck."

"Mister Lehmbeck, I'm sorry. Miss Tate is on the phone. Didn't her assistant show up on time?"

"Yes, she did, but I have a few questions for Leah." I closed my eyes praying the girl either got Leah or put me through to her voicemail.

"You could always try her personal cell number."

"I already did, she isn't answering that."

"I'm sorry, sir, you can always try emailing her. Is there anything else I can help you with?"

"No, thanks." I hung up the phone. I was beyond irritated that she didn't show up this morning.

I sat through my meetings trying hard to focus on the task at hand. Instead, my phone wouldn't stop going off. Every time I looked at it, another question from Susan sat on my screen. Questions I couldn't answer because Leah was supposed to be in charge and answering them—not me. *Leah would be there in forty minutes and she gave Susan all the instructions she needed, my ass.*

I shortened the second meeting, my phone still going off, now with questions from my own clients as well as from Susan. I left the building in a rush and headed home.

I pulled up to the house, noting furniture was still being unloaded out of trucks. When I walked inside, Susan stood in the living room directing people. "Everything okay now?" I asked.

"Yes, sorry about all the questions. Leah finally arrived and everything is going fine now."

I looked around—it was beginning to look and feel like a real home. "Where is Leah?"

"She is upstairs," she answered as she crossed another thing off her list and directed two men where to put the item they were carrying.

I looked toward the stairs and smiled at Susan, excusing myself. I climbed the stairs and found Leah in my bedroom making the bed. "Hey," I called out as I entered the almost finished room.

"Hey," she said letting out a breath. "Sorry I wasn't here for the start of everything, I needed to speak with the appliance company, they were showing the wrong model fridge coming in."

"I see. Listen, do you have a minute, I want to talk to you."

"Now isn't a good time, Logan. I need to make sure things keep moving along."

"It will only take a few minutes."

"Miss Tate, I need your help," Susan called from downstairs.

"See she needs me," Leah said placing the last pillow on the bed before leaving the room. I stood there looking after her.

The rest of the afternoon went that way. I would corner Leah somewhere and she would find any excuse to get away from me or Susan would appear out of thin air. The next day started the same way, only I got so tired of it I ended up leaving the house.

At six I pulled into the driveway in time to see the last truck pull away. The only two vehicles remaining were Leah and Susan's. I hurried into the house, hoping to catch her before she left.

Susan and Leah were in the kitchen going over one the final plans. "Can you make sure that everything is in place according to this please?" I watched as she handed over the plan to Susan. "Oh, and check to make sure that the peach in the blinds matched the peach in the duvet, please." She was beautiful when she took control. I leaned up against the door frame waiting for Susan to leave.

Finally, Leah was alone, studying something that sat in front of her. I cleared my throat letting her know I was there.

"Logan, we are just finishing up. We should be out of here shortly."

"No rush," I said walking over to her. I went up behind her and placed my arms on either side of her. "I'd like to speak with you in private," I whispered into her ear.

"Logan, please, now isn't the time."

I went to whisper something else into her ear when Susan walked into the room. "Oh my, I am so sorry, I didn't mean to interrupt."

"Don't be silly, Susan," Leah said as she stepped away from me. "I was just showing Logan something. Is everything good to go?"

Susan nodded looking at me and back at Leah.

"We should get going." Leah packed up everything that was on the counter and shoved it into her briefcase then she and Susan walked to the door.

"Miss Tate, you will be here for the magazine shoot, correct?"

"Yes, sir. Thursday at nine. I will see you then."

27
Leah

I checked my makeup for the fifth time before walking out the door. I had been able to avoid speaking to Logan all week. I knew it pissed Logan off, but I struggled to handle how I was feeling and that kiss we had shared recently hadn't left my thoughts.

I smoothed my skirt and quickly wrapped a scarf around my neck then, for the sixth time in five minutes, I checked my hair and makeup. As soon as I was satisfied, I headed down to my car and started the drive to Logan's. I decided that as soon as the shoot was over, I was flying home for the weekend. I needed to get out of this city for a while and away from Logan.

I drove up the driveway and parked in beside his truck. I shut the engine off and sat there for a moment taking in everything. I had hit this design out of the park, fully impressing Mary with the whole design too. She had come to see it yesterday with Susan and had told me so. She was thrilled that it would be featured in the magazine and that the magazine wanted me to be part of it.

"I seriously cannot think of a better designer to represent Preston Interior Design," she had said as she continued her way through Logan's home. I should have been proud of what I had accomplished, but instead I felt empty.

I took a deep breath, climbed out of my car and slowly walked to the front door. I hadn't even knocked before Logan had pulled the door open and stood before me. He wore loose fitting khakis and a tight white t-shirt that showed off every muscle in his upper body. I felt that familiar ache and a rush of heat between my legs as he smiled his classic "come fuck me" smile while leaning against the door frame.

"Morning."

"Morning. I hope everything is to your satisfaction?" I asked.

"Better than I could imagine," he said his eyes traveling the length of my body.

"Glad to hear. What time are they coming?"

"The crew should be here in ten minutes, come in and have a cup of coffee."

I slipped my shoes off, then I followed him into the kitchen, smelling his delicious scent the whole way. I was quiet as I watched his forearm flex when he poured me a cup and handed me the mug, our fingers touching as I took it from him.

We both sat down at the table and each took a sip. Our eyes met and held. "About that night . . ." we both said in unison and then we smiled at one another.

"You go first," I said waiting for him to speak.

"No, ladies first."

"Logan, I meant what I said back home. Sex with you was amazing but I can't do this with you. I know you are only after a fling or whatever you call it, but for me, my clock is ticking, and I want and need to find the real thing. I don't want to waste your time or mine."

As the words fell from my mouth, I wished I could take some back as I watched the reaction that fell across his face. It was like I had gutted him in a matter of two seconds.

"After the shoot today, I'm heading home for the weekend. I need to figure out what I am doing with myself and this job. I'm going to ask that you don't call me or come home too."

"Leah, I—" The doorbell rang interrupting whatever it was he was going to say. He looked at his watch. "Fuck, she's here already."

"Go get the door, I'll tidy up in here." I smiled at him.

He looked at me and said, "Just wait a minute—" The door-bell broke into his words again.

"Logan, go, they're waiting." I got up from the table and rinsed our mugs before putting them in the dishwasher, ignoring the fact that he stood looking at me waiting to say something.

I looked around, wishing that along with Logan, that this home could be mine too. I had put the finishing touches on his beautiful design and standing here with him in this kitchen, being wrapped in his arms last night, I felt complete. I quickly wiped the tears that built in my eyes, I couldn't afford to have my makeup run.

Jean walked into the living room and I watched from the kitchen as her crew set up their equipment. Jean had pulled Logan aside to speak to him about the process for today, I stayed in the kitchen out of the way. I knew she wanted to include a small section about me and the firm to go along with the article.

I was hoping to get my part done and over with first so I could get out of here. I sat at the table and checked my emails. The bustle of everyone in the living room as things were set up was a little louder than I wanted. Over it all, I could still hear Logan and Jean talking.

Soon Jean came into the kitchen. "Hello, Miss Tate. It's nice to meet you. You have done a wonderful job with everything. The house looks stunning."

"Thank you." I smiled. "If it's not too much to ask, could we possibly get my stuff done and out of the way first? I have a flight to catch."

"I wanted to talk to you about that. We would like you to partake in all the photos as well."

I couldn't believe my ears and I looked to Logan. He stood there straight-faced and shrugged his shoulders. "I . . . that is unnecessary."

"No, believe me it's necessary. The model we had chosen to help with the shoot fell ill at the last moment and canceled," she said firmly. I could see there would be no arguing with this woman, so I shut my mouth and followed them both into the living room where we began an entire day of photos. We worked tirelessly to get the right shots done in every room. When the last shot had been taken, Jean began directing her crew and I excused myself, Logan following closely behind me.

"Leah, aren't you going to stay for the interview?" he asked catching up to me.

"I told you, I have a flight to catch."

"But I really need to talk to you alone, it's important," he said brushing away the strand of hair that had fallen into my eyes.

"There is nothing more to say, Logan. Good luck with everything. You have designed a beautiful home, and some woman will be very lucky to have you." I leaned into him and placed a long lingering goodbye kiss on his lips. It was wrong to do that to him, but I felt it was necessary for my own closure.

"Logan, I would like to do the interview now," Jean called from the living room as some of the crew walked by us.

I took my purse and coat from the hall closet, smiled at Logan, thanked Jean, and walked out the front door. I knew he wouldn't make a scene with everyone around. I was already fighting back tears when I felt his hand on my arm. "Wait."

I looked up at him. "What?"

He said nothing, as he leaned into me. I put my hand to his chest, stopping him from coming any closer.

"Logan, I meant what I said. All or nothing. I have to go, and Jean is waiting for you." I kissed him one final time and then I turned and made my way to the car, swallowing hard as I listened to the gravel crunch below my feet. I looked back. Logan stood watching me as I climbed into the car. I started the engine and quickly backed out letting the floodgate of tears open once again as I drove down the driveway.

My plane landed shortly after one. I glanced at my watch to check the current time. I had called my mother last night asking her if she had gotten my email. She told me she had run right out to the store and picked up the magazine and that she was so proud of me and what I had done. I had asked her if she would mind telling Leah it was available, she hadn't been answering my calls or texts again.

"I'll admit, Logan, I'm a little worried about her," she whispered into the phone. "She arrived home last night, this is the second visit this month and she has barely left her room since she got here. Joe is beside himself. She isn't herself. Do you know what happened to her?"

"I have a feeling I do," I mumbled more to myself, mentally beating myself up for not telling her how I really felt before she got on that plane the night of the photo shoot. I had even debated following her to the airport, but Jean had taken up too much of my time. All I knew was that I wanted to be with Leah, and I had to let her know it.

"Is it serious, Logan? Did something happen to her?" she asked.

I knew Joe was probably sitting beside her praying I would tell them so he knew how to help his daughter, but there was nothing they could do, this was all up to me. I figured if I wanted his daughter, I deserved whatever words he would have to say, and that they should be said to my face and not over the phone.

"I don't think it's anything to worry about, Mom, I think she is just overworked, perhaps a little homesick." I lied.

"I hope you're right. Well, you're coming home will do her good, I think. She told me she did a fantastic job on your home. Are you happy with it?"

"I couldn't be more pleased." Mom was right, she had done a fantastic job designing my home. There was only one thing missing, and I hoped that the missing object would agree with me and come home.

"Do me a favor, Mom, don't tell her I am coming."

"Why on earth not?"

"Are you alone, Mom?"

"Yes."

"Joe isn't there?"

"Logan, what is going on. Why would it matter if Joe was here or not?" she asked me, alarm building in her voice.

I debated how to tell her what happened. I mean it's not everyday someone falls in love with their stepsister. "Are you sitting down, Mom?"

"Logan." Her voice came over the phone a cross between irritated and annoyed.

"She came home because of me."

"What? What did you do?"

I took a deep breath and replied, "We slept together, I'm in love with her, Mom. I was horrible to her."

"I don't understand."

I couldn't tell if I pissed my mother off or if she were shocked.

"Logan, when did this happen?" she asked.

"The weekend of your anniversary. I told her I didn't want anything serious, when I was just confused as to how I really felt. I need her, Mom."

"Oh, Logan . . ."

"I know, but please help me make things right, Mom. I need her, she is my missing piece," I begged into the phone.

Mom agreed to help me and together we devised a plan. She wouldn't tell Leah I was coming home. Once I arrived, she would call Leah down from her room to show her the magazine article, which I had demanded be titled "It Was All or Nothing." I hoped she would see through that title, but then maybe she wouldn't. I had asked Jean to use only the pictures that were of Leah and me together so that as she read the article perhaps, she would put two and two together.

The plan was for Mom and Leah to be looking through the magazine together then I would surprise Leah from behind. Mom had said she would talk to Joe for me. I prayed that everything was all right and Joe wouldn't kill me when he saw me.

I made my way through the airport toward the car rental counter, and ten minutes later I was sitting behind the wheel of my rental car. I quickly sent a text to my mom and was on my way to the house. My hands shook on the wheel as I sat at a red light just around the corner from my girl. My girl, I loved the sound of that. I couldn't believe how nervous I was.

Within a few minutes I pulled into the driveway, Joe's vehicle parked behind my mom's. I went in quietly through the kitchen door and found my mom with her head in the oven basting a chicken and roasted potatoes.

"Honey! You're home!" she whispered as soon as she saw me. She dropped the baster in the sink and ran over wrapping her arms around my neck.

"Hey, Mom." I hugged her back, my stomach literally turning at what I was about to do. The thought of knowing the real answer from Leah within minutes was playing with my mind.

"Just be quiet, Leah is in the other room. I've been waiting for you," she whispered. "Don't worry, Joe is okay with it." She winked.

For whatever reason the news of that eased a lot of my nerves. "I'll warn you now, she isn't in the best of moods, but you stay here while I go show her the article."

I nodded, letting go of my mother and heading to the fridge for a bottle of water. I sat just inside the doorway to the kitchen and listened as my mom went into the living room, first picking the magazine up off the counter and taking it with her.

"Oh, Leah, I forgot to tell you, look what I found at the store? I figured you would like to see this."

I listened to her murmured reply, "That's nice, I'll look at it later."

"But, Leah, honey, you need to see this, they have recognized you for doing such a beautiful job. Don't you want to see it?"

"No, Anna, not right now, please, I will look at it later. Mary already emailed me about it." She let out a sniffle.

"Here let me refill your tea." Mom came back into the kitchen carrying her cup and put the kettle on. "I tried."

"Try harder, much harder," I said through clenched teeth. I had just flown halfway across the country, and I wasn't going home without her.

As soon as the kettle boiled Mom poured the hot water over the fresh tea bag and carried it back into the living room where she stopped as soon as she set eyes on Leah. She waved her hand for me to see. I poked my head around the corner careful to keep out of Leah's line of sight. She sat with the magazine in her lap, her hand over her mouth, tears in her eyes as she flipped through the article.

"Leah, what is it?" I watched Mom go over to Leah and sit the cup down on the end table before kneeling before her.

"It's just . . . it's nothing. Can you get me the phone?" she asked through fresh tears.

"What for, honey."

"I need to call Logan. This is humiliating! The way this article reads it's like they think we are together! What the hell was he thinking?"

"Leah, calm down. I don't think he . . ."

"No. Don't tell me to calm down. It's no wonder Mary emailed me. This hurts, Anna."

"What, honey, what hurts?"

I swallowed the lump that sat in my throat, listening to her cry because she thought I would purposely hurt her. It was killing me. She needed to read between the lines of that stupid article and stop being so fucking stubborn.

"Logan. This wasn't supposed to happen, but I've been in love with him for years. I tried so hard to get his attention, and he never noticed until he came back for your anniversary. He noticed me then and made damn sure he took what he wanted and then spit it back at me." Her sobs were heartbreaking.

"Leah . . ."

"Anna, give me the phone. I'm done."

I was finished listening to her cry. I took a deep breath and stepped into the living room. My mom was still crouched down in front of her, her hands on Leah's knees. Joe stood at the base of the stairs looking utterly afraid to step into the room for fear of getting yelled at. I said nothing I just stood there watching.

"Leah, honey, please . . ."

"No, Anna, your son has done enough damage, he has broken my heart. I can't do this anymore. I'm going to be the laughing stock of the office. After I talk to him, I'm calling the design firm and I am moving back home. There is no way I can face those people after this."

"You don't have to call me," I said, my voice echoing in the room. "I can clearly see my plan has failed and that you haven't read between the lines, Leah."

She looked up at me, a look of shock and surprise and then hurt on her face. "Logan, what the hell, this article, it will get me fired."

"You just said you were going to quit. So what does it matter? And why would you get fired?"

"Because, Logan, it looks like . . ."

"Looks like what?"

Leah looked down at the magazine and flipped back to the start of the article. "The way it's laid out, and with the pictures, it looks like I conspired with you to get this job and into this shoot. She's made it look as if we are together, for god's sake."

"What does the headline read, Leah?"

"It Was All or Nothing," she read aloud looking down at the page in front of her.

"That's right. What is the significance of those words in relation to us?"

She sniffled, wiping her nose with a tissue my mom had handed to her and shrugged her shoulders.

"What were the words you said to me the weekend we were together?"

"It has to be all or nothing."

"Well . . ."

She looked up at me, a realization coming over her face, a cute little smile forming on her lips. Anna stood up from where she was kneeling and looked to Leah and smiled.

"Really, Logan? For real?" she asked between sobs.

"For real."

She stood there a deep flush growing on her cheeks as the realization hit.

"Well, what are you waiting for?" I asked.

She got up out of the chair, dropped the magazine to the floor, crossed the room and fell right into my arms. I wrapped mine around hers and pulled her tightly against me, comforting her. Mom snuck by me and I heard her tell Joe to come with her and leave us be. As I held Leah in my arms, breathing in her familiar scent, I felt lighter than I had in months.

"I'm sorry I took so long to figure things out, but I realized something the other day. The only thing missing to make my life complete is the perfect girl." I pulled away from her to look at her face. "You. You're my missing piece. I want to spend my life with you. Everything points to you," I whispered in her ear as she rested her head on my shoulder.

She pulled back and looked up into my eyes, her green eyes

dancing as they always had done when she had looked at me. "Thank god, Logan, because I love you."

"I love you too, Gingersnap." I didn't wait, I devoured her mouth, my tongue darting in between those perfect lips.

A short while later, we pulled into the parking lot of the nearest hotel. There was no way I would be able to take what was mine with Mom and Joe in the next room. I went into the lobby and rented a room for the night. Together, hand in hand, we walked to the room and I slid the key into the lock.

As soon as we were through the door, I pinned her against the wall and pulled her t-shirt over her head. I couldn't wait to get my hands on her. I found the clasp of her bra and quickly flicked it open, the material falling away from her perfect sized breasts. I kissed down her neck, taking a nipple into my mouth, swirling my tongue around then taking it between my teeth gently biting. She let out a soft sexy moan, so I did it to the other one. I stood back up meeting her mouth, grinding my hips against her as I pressed her harder into the wall.

She gripped me through my pants and ran her hand the length of the me, squeezing and stroking my hardness through my jeans. It was all I could do to hold back, if she kept it up it wouldn't be long before I blew my load into my pants. I ripped her hands away and picked her up, carrying her to the bed where I lay her down.

I pulled at the button on her jeans, opening them and unzipping the zipper. I got a peek at her red panties while I pulled her jeans off her, then I slowly inched her panties down her legs. I quickly unzipped my pants, letting them fall to the floor while her eyes scanned down to my hardened cock, watching it spring free. I placed my knee on the bed between her legs, making my way up her body. I braced myself on my elbow and crashed into her mouth.

Her hand grabbed my cock and started stroking me, she ran her thumb over the head, rubbing the bead of pre-cum that had gathered there. "Fuck, Leah," I breathed out as I ran my fingers through her wetness, concentrating on her clit. I slid two fingers into her, relishing in the feeling of her tightness.

"Logan, please, make love to me," she moaned into my mouth.

"Fuck me," I said dropping my head down beside her shoulder in frustration.

"What? What is it?"

"I forgot the fucking condoms, Leah."

She rolled onto her side and looked into my eyes. "I don't care, Logan, I want you to make love to me. I want to feel you inside me."

She lay back down, and I propped myself up on my elbow. "Are you sure?"

"Yes." She looked up at me shyly. I gave myself a couple of pumps and ran my cock through her center finally pushing myself all the way inside her. She let out a full moan as I buried myself into her.

I felt her tightening around me, so I slowed down, slowly pumping into her hard and deep. She felt incredible as she hugged my cock and her fingers dug into me running her nails down my back. Hearing her moans getting louder, I reached between us, running my fingers over her clit as I continued to pound into her. I felt a rush of heat as she came all over me, calling out my name. I felt the familiar throbbing start just before I let go, pouring myself into her.

I collapsed on her breathing hard as she placed soft kisses on my shoulder. Once I gathered myself, I pulled out of her and rolled onto my back pulling her into me. She rested her head on my shoulder, slowing her breathing as she relaxed against me.

I checked out the front window and then glanced at the clock. It was almost two, Dad and Anna were coming to visit for Christmas. It was the first time they had come to Boston at Christmas time, and we were excited to have them stay with us.

"Are they here yet?" I heard Logan ask from behind me.

"No. I thought you were putting the finishing touches on the McGill project?" I said taking a sip of my soda water.

"I'm working on it."

"Well, get back to it, they are not here yet. To be honest, I don't know what is taking them so long, their plane landed at twelve."

"Probably traffic. You know what it's like this time of the year."

I went back to the counter where I had a roast sitting in a pan and finished putting the slices of onion in with the meat and sprinkled the seasoning over it. I covered it and placed it into the already hot oven.

"Do you think they will be happy at the news?"

Logan had asked me to marry him last week over dinner at one of the top restaurants in Boston. He had even gotten down on one knee causing everyone in the restaurant to turn and look at us as he proposed. It was the most romantic thing ever, and then we had come home and made love for hours. After I called Jenna and told her the news, we both laughed as her shrill squeal poured through the phone.

"I think they will love it." He came up behind me, wrapped

me in his arms and placed little kisses along the back of my neck making me laugh. "However, I think they will like our other news better," he whispered as he continued kissing me.

"What the fact we are finally opening our own design firm?" After they had published the article, things went crazy for us. We both had more work than we could handle and Logan and two other architects he worked with branched off and opened their own firm. I was in such high demand at Preston that I could barely keep up, and then Logan suggested I should join his firm and take over the interior design side of things. I gave my notice at Preston just before we closed for Christmas and I posted an ad for designers to join me at Lehmbeck Designs.

Logan laughed as he placed his hand along the flat of my stomach. "You know what news I'm referring to," he said taking my mouth.

I broke the kiss. "We shouldn't say anything yet, just in case."

"In case of what?"

"They say to wait three months, just to make sure everything is fine."

"Then why did you tell me?"

I looked at him and laughed and started cutting up potatoes. "Don't be ridiculous, Logan, of course I had to tell you, you were there."

"Well, I can't wait to share that news either," he said pouting as he pushed me against the wall and met my lips.

I heard a car pull up to the house and looked out the window over Logan's shoulder to see Anna climb out of the car and look around at the house all decorated in Christmas lights. "They're here."

"They will have to wait, I need to make love to you right now," he said pulling my hand down between us and placing it on his hard cock.

"Put that away, Logan, your mother is here." I laughed pushing him away and then kissing him quickly.

We both looked to one another and smiled. "Let's just hit them with the news of the engagement first, okay. I don't want to kill my father at the same time," I whispered into his ear, kissing him on the cheek.

"I don't get it, why would that news kill your father?"

"Logan, you know why." I had always promised my dad I would get married before I had a baby. It wasn't going to happen that way.

"So, we get married next week." He looked at me his eyes full of mischief.

"You're crazy, I can't pull a wedding together in a week. No one could."

"Yes, you can. I need nothing elaborate, just something like Mom and Joe. I already know I love you; I don't need to announce it to the world with a big show."

I smiled and threw my arms around his neck kissing him. "I love you too." He took my hand in his and together we walked to the front door to greet our guests.

<<<< ***The End*** >>>>

Note from the author

Dear Readers,

I would like to thank you for taking the time to read *Bad Company*. I hope you enjoyed Leah and Logan's story.

If you did, I would love it if you would drop me a review. Reviews are important to me; I love to hear what my readers think.

I wanted to give you a little update. I have been working hard on the remainder of the Malone Brother's series. I have titles for the other two books in the series, along with release dates. I also have a couple of other releases planned for this year. To be kept up to date with the progress of these titles and to be notified of release dates, make sure you add the following to your Goodreads TBR. You do not want to miss what I have coming up for the rest of 2019!

<u>Coming Soon</u>

August 2019: Malone Brothers Book 3,
Bryce: http://bit.ly/HistoHold
October 2019 Dagger: http://bit.ly/GRDagger
November/December 2019 Untitled Holiday Romance: http://bit.ly/GRHolidayRomance

About S.L. STERLING

S.L. Sterling had been an avid reader since she was a child, often found getting lost in books. Today if she isn't writing or plotting, she can be found buried in a romance novel. S.L. Sterling lives with her husband and dog in Northern Ontario.

Join my Street Team
Sterlings Silver Sapphires:
http://bit.ly/SterlingsSapphires

Facebook: http://bit.ly/BeholdthePowerofRomance
Follow me on Bookbub: http://bit.ly/SLSterlingBookbub
Instagram: http://bit.ly/SLSterlingInstagram
Goodreads: http://bit.ly/SLSterlingGoodreads
Pinterest: http://bit.ly/SLSterlingPinterest
Twitter: http://bit.ly/SLSterlingTwitter
Newsletter: http://bit.ly/SLSterlingNewsletter
Website: www.authorslsterling.com

Other books by
S.L. STERLING

It Was Always You

On A Silent Night

The Malone Brothers

A Kiss Beneath the Stars (The Malone Brothers 1)

In Your Arms (The Malone Brothers 2)